* * * * * * *

Marcie watched him as he disappeared from sight. She tried to call out to him, to beg for his help, to plead with him not to leave her. But no matter how hard she tried, she could not force the words from her lips. She heard the car start. She was sure that he was going to drive off and leave her there to freeze to death. Panic began to well up in her. Even though she was afraid of him, she was still able to comprehend that if someone did not help her soon she would
die all alone right there in the parking lot.

Just then, the man returned carrying a bright red and black plaid car blanket. He knelt down, brushed the snow from her coat, then carefully wrapped the blanket around her shoulders and over her legs. Sliding his arms under her, he picked her up and gently carried her to the car. Opening the door, he set her in on the seat and tucked the blanket around her as best he could before shutting the door.

* * * * * * *

Other Large Print Editions by J.E. Terrall

Western Short Stories
   The Old West
   The Frontier
   Untamed Land
   Tales from the Territory
   Frontier Justice

Western Novels
   Conflict in Elkhorn Valley
   The Valley Ranch War

Other Novels by J.E. Terrall
   Sing for Me
   Return to Me
   The Return Home

SING FOR ME

**by
J. E. Terrall**

ISBN: 978-0-9994727-6-7

This is a work of fiction. Names, characters, and incidents are either a product of the author's imagination or are used fictitiously, and any resemblance to actual persons, living or dead, is purely coincidental.

Printed in the United States of America

Large Print Edition printed by www.createspace

SING FOR ME

To
Valda Rossman

PROLOGUE

"Marcie, don't go far. We'll be ready to test the lighting and sound equipment soon."

Marcie Roberts did not answer the stagehand. She simply nodded to let him know that she had heard him as she walked toward the big overhead doors in the back of the arena. It was the same thing every night, night after night. She never had any time for herself.

Marcie was feeling very lonely, a feeling that had become far too familiar to her lately. She looked around and saw a dozen people she knew, but they were all too busy to notice her. For the past four years, she had been doing the same thing. She would be in one town one night, and another town the next night. She never had time to see the country, to go shopping with a friend or to visit with the local people. She certainly never had time to get to really know anyone.

Slipping her arms into her raincoat, she stepped out the back door of the large arena and looked out over the huge parking lot. It was just beginning to snow. She did not know what she was looking for, but there had to be something interesting out there. Something that would stimulate her senses and make her feel alive again. There had to be something new for her to discover. Whatever it was it had to be better than what she was leaving behind.

CHAPTER ONE

It was early December and Christmas was only three weeks away. Thick dark clouds hung over the city like a thick wet blanket. The lights of the city cast an eerie glow off the clouds as large wet flakes of snow began to fall. At first, they melted almost as soon as they touched the pavement. Only those landing on the grass or other foliage seemed to be able to survive. Gradually, the temperature fell and the snowflakes cooled the pavement, then the snow began to stick everywhere. Winter had come late this year, but it looked like it was finally here to stay.

In a very short time, the cars in Denver's Mile High Stadium parking lot were covered with wet sticky snow. It would not be long before the Denver Bronco fans would be pouring out of the stadium to their cars. They would clean the snow off the windshields and drive home, as they had done so many times in the past. But, for the moment, the parking lot of the huge stadium was almost completely void of people. In the background, one could hear the sounds of the fans as they cheered on their home team.

A slim, well-built woman walked out of one of the side doors of McNichol's arena and looked out across the giant parking lot toward the stadium. She wrapped the thin raincoat tightly around her as the first few snowflakes touched her face. As she began walking across the parking lot, she did not seem to notice the cold or the wet snow as it brushed against her cheeks, touched her long eyelashes and melted in her soft hair.

The clicking sound of her high heels on the asphalt carried out over the vast parking lot. The further away from the arena she went, the faster she walked. Before long the woman was running through the parking lot, to where she did not know.

Miss Marcie Roberts did not seem to know where she was headed. Yet, she was determined to get away from where she had been. She was not even sure what she was running away from or to. By the time she reached the far side of the stadium, she had been running for some distance. She was not used to the altitude of the mile high city, and it was taking its toll on her.

She stopped and leaned against a car as she tried to catch her breath. Looking back toward the arena, she could not see anyone. No one had followed her, at least not yet. She had gotten away, but away from what and for how long? Where had she gone? Where was she going?

The wet snow had matted Marcie's hair. Loose strands of her hair were clinging to her face. The cold evening air was slowly beginning to penetrate the thin raincoat causing her to shiver. She was not only cold and wet, she was now frightened. But no matter how frightened she was, she knew in her own mind that she could not return to the arena, she would not return to the arena. She could not stand to live like that any more. She wouldn't do it. Life was too short to live from town to town day after day.

It was only after she caught her breath and had taken a minute or so to look around that she realized she had gone the wrong way. She had run into a corner. There was a high fence separating her from a busy Interstate highway, leaving her with nowhere to go, except back in the direction that she had come.

She again looked back toward the arena. Now she could see two rather large men in heavy coats walking among the rows of cars in the arena parking lot. They were looking for something. She instinctively knew that they were looking for her. It was only a matter of time before they would go back to the arena and get more help so they could spread out their search to cover the entire parking lot.

Marcie quickly looked around. Parked near the concrete retaining wall was a Jeep Cherokee. Unlike the other cars around it, it was backed into the parking space. It looked as if it might provide her with some small measure of shelter from the sharp wind and bitter cold, as well as a place to hide. It was probably not the best hiding place for her, but it would have to do until she had a chance to think. She moved around behind the Jeep and crouched down against the retaining wall.

The coat she wore was not heavy enough for tonight's weather. She tried to wrap her coat around her legs, but it did not help much. She was wet and so cold that her teeth were beginning to chatter uncontrollably.

She started to sob as she began to realize the world she had known as a child, the home she had once known, would never be hers again. She had sold her family values for fame and money, only to find that fame and money weren't what she really wanted.

Right now, she was not sure what she wanted. The only thing she was sure of was that she was very cold, very wet and very much alone. She could not remember ever feeling so much alone, and it frightened her.

It continued to grow colder as the evening wore on. Her toes and legs were starting to lose their feeling. She could not stop shaking. Her shaking was so violent that she was not sure she could go back to the arena even if she wanted to. She did not think that she could even stand up without help.

Her mind began to wonder. She could no longer think clearly. Her thoughts turned to what had been a better time for her. A time when she did not have the pressures she faced now. Marcie remembered the day of her high school graduation. It was a time when she had nothing to worry about and no real responsibilities. Everything looked great and her future looked bright. Yet the day that she had been offered her first singing contract turned out to be the very day that her life had changed, forever.

The cold had begun to penetrate her body. Gradually, her mind became clouded and she faded in and out of awareness of her surroundings. With her mind wondering so much, and the new fallen snow covering the parking lot, she did not hear the footsteps of someone approaching.

As Tony Beckman walked around to the driver's side of his Jeep, he sorted through his keys for the one that would open the door. As he did, he happened to notice a shoe near the back of his car but he paid little attention to it. He simply opened the door and got in. As he put the key into the ignition, something in the depths of his mind told him to stop and take minute to look behind his Jeep before he drove away.

Tony got back out and walked to the rear of his car. The last thing he expected to find was someone huddled down in the snow, but there on the ground was a woman. She was wet and half-covered with snow. If it had not been for her shaking and the slight vapor of her breath in the cold night air, he would have thought she was dead. It was immediately clear to him that she was not dressed for this kind of weather. He knelt down beside her and reached out to touch her cheek.

"Miss, Miss?" he called to her.

Deep down in the recesses of her mind, Marcie heard the man's voice. It sounded so far off that she didn't respond to it. She felt something pleasantly warm on her face and slowly opened her eyes. It took a second or two for it to register in her mind that someone was kneeling over her and his hand was touching her cheek. She tried to scream and move away from him, but she could do neither. She just looked up at him with eyes that showed her fear.

"Don't be afraid. Let me help you," the man said.

His voice sounded gentle and caring. There was something deep inside her that told her not to resist him, to let him help, but she was frightened.

Tony took his hand away from her. Her eyes reminded him of a small puppy that was cold, wet and afraid. The big difference here was, she was no puppy. This was a grown woman who was wet, frightened and slowly but surely freezing to death. She needed help and needed it before she suffered from frostbite. He was sure she was not only frightened, but most likely suffering from hypothermia already.

When Tony reached out to her, she tried to back away again, but she was unable to move. He remembered there was a wool car blanket in the back seat of his car. If he got the blanket and wrapped her in it, she might understand that he was only trying to help her.

Marcie watched him as he disappeared from sight. She tried to call out to him, to beg for his help, to plead with him not to leave her.

But no matter how hard she tried, she could not force the words from her lips. She heard the car start. She was sure that he was going to drive off and leave her there to freeze to death. Panic began to well up in her. Even though she was afraid of him, she was still able to comprehend that if someone did not help her soon she would die all alone right there in the parking lot.

Just then, the man returned carrying a bright red and black plaid car blanket. He knelt down, brushed the snow from her coat, then carefully wrapped the blanket around her shoulders and over her legs. Sliding his arms under her, he picked her up and gently carried her to the car. Opening the door, he set her in on the seat and tucked the blanket around her as best he could before shutting the door.

She watched him through the windshield as he cleaned the snow off the glass and away from the headlights. It didn't take long before Marcie began to feel the warm air from the car's heater on her feet. As he got into the car and shut the door, she looked over at him. Her mind was filled with confusion, yet there was once again a tiny bit of hope.

"I'm going to take you to a hospital. They will get you warmed up."

Tony put the car in gear and started for the exit of the parking lot. Marcie saw several people near the back door of the arena looking out over the parking lot. She turned her face away in the hope that they would not see her.

Tony was trying to figure this woman out. She did not look like a person who was homeless. The raincoat and shoes she was wearing looked to be rather expensive. They were not the kind of clothing a homeless person would wear. Although she was wet and her hair was a mess, he was sure that she was normally a well-groomed person.

He wondered what she was doing in the parking lot. What was it that could have frighten this woman so much that she would risk her life to get away by trying to hide in a parking lot during a snowstorm? Had someone dumped her there? She didn't seem to be injured. Was she running away from someone? He had a dozen or more questions for her; but since she was not talking, there was no way for him to get answers. It suddenly occurred to Tony that she might not be able to talk.

Tony turned out onto Federal Boulevard and started driving toward 17th Street. If he remembered correctly, there was a hospital on 17th Street not too far from the stadium. He turned on 17th and headed west.

"Please, don't... take....me to....a hos....pital."

Her voice was so low he could hardly hear her over the engine and the heater fan. He glanced at her. It was the first time she had said anything. She was still very cold and still shaking, but at least she was beginning to talk.

"I think you should go to the hospital. They will be able to help you."

"Please," she begged.

Her eyes pleaded with him. Tony was not sure what to do now. If she was suffering from hypothermia, and he was sure she was, he needed to get her warm. To get her warm, he needed to get something warm in her stomach and some warm, dry clothes for her.

"Where do you want me to take you?"

Marcie just looked at him, but did not answer. If she went back to her hotel room, she would end up going home for a while, but would soon be back out on the road again. She certainly did not want to go back to the arena.

"Do you have some place to go?"

What Marcie wanted was to go home, back to that small town in southern Ohio where she had grown up. She just looked at him, unable to think clearly enough to give him a clear answer.

He pulled his car over to the curb and stopped. Tony was rapidly growing frustrated and worried about her.

"I can't help you if you won't talk to me. Please, tell me how I can help you."

Marcie looked into his eyes. This man seemed truly sincere about wanting to help her. His eyes seemed gentle and warm. There was something about this man that told her she could trust him, that she would be safe with him. That same something from deep in the recess of her mind also told her that he would not take advantage of her. He would not tell her what to do and when to do it, like her promoter and so many others had been doing for so long that it had become almost a habit for them.

Tony watched her as she tried to think. He waited for an answer. What was wrong with taking her to his home, he thought? At least there he could get her warmed up and into some dry clothes. He wasn't sure he should suggest it, but he couldn't just sit here and watch her shiver. He had to do something.

He was sure she was frightened and the idea of going to his house might frighten her even more. Yet, in looking at her in those wet clothes and shivering while he sat there doing nothing was not the answer either. He had to do something and do it soon, before she ended up with pneumonia or something worse.

"Listen. I have a place not far from here. I can take you there and get you something warm to eat and find some dry clothes for you to wear. Would that be okay?"

Tony had tried to choose his words carefully. He wanted her to understand he was only trying to help her, and that he wanted nothing from her. He again waited for her to respond to his suggestion, but she just stared at him with those beautiful, but frightened blue eyes.

"Damn it, woman. I can't help you if you won't talk to me. Is it okay to go to my place, or do I take you to the hospital?" he demanded in frustration.

He had a nice face and seemed to be really worried about her, she thought. After what seemed like a very long time, Marcie replied.

"Not.... the.... hospital...please," she said, her eyes pleading.

Marcie did not say she was willing to go to his house, but she could not think of any other place where she would not be found. What she needed was some place to get warm and to have time to think, and thinking was difficult for her at this moment. She had to admit to herself that she needed his help, somebody's help.

Marcie was not sure her decision was a good one, but she did not have much choice. If she went to a hospital, she would be found. If she went back to her hotel, she certainly would be found. She realized she had little choice but to trust this man.

Tony pulled away from the curb and made a U turn in the middle of the street. After driving for several minutes, he pulled up to the curb in front of a rather large two-story home across the street from Washington Park. He shut off the engine, got out, ran around to the other side of his car and opened the door.

The snow was already about two inches deep and it was still coming down hard. Tony reached in, slid his arms under her and picked her up, blanket and all. She wrapped her arms around his neck as he lifted her out of the car. Pushing the car door closed with his hip, he then carried her up the sidewalk to the large porch.

Once on the porch, he stood her up. Supporting her with one arm, Tony reached into his coat pocket for the key to the house. As soon as the door was opened, he put his arms around her and led her into the house. He gently kicked the door closed behind them.

"I have a spare bedroom upstairs. There's a bathroom right off the bedroom. You can stay there for tonight."

Marcie let him help her up the stairs. Her legs were still very weak and she was not sure she could get up the stairs without his help. Her feet still tingled from the cold and feeling had not completely returned to them.

"Here we go," he said as he pushed open the bedroom door.

Tony turned on the light as they entered the bedroom. The room was nicely done in soft colors of blues and greens. The bed was a queen size bed with a large, thick comforter. It looked warm and very inviting.

"You might feel better if you take a warm shower. I'm afraid I don't have any women's clothes, but I can get you a pair of my flannel pajamas and a robe. They won't fit you very well, but they will keep you warm."

Standing in the middle of the room, still wrapped in his car blanket, she smiled at him. It was a small smile, but it was the first time she had shown any expression of hope or any expression of gratitude.

"There are towels in the bathroom. I'll go get you something to wear. Will you be okay?"

She nodded that she would be fine. He smiled and started to leave the room. At the door, he stopped and turned toward her.

"You can leave your wet things in the bathroom. I'll go fix you something to eat while you shower and warm up. Just call if you need anything. I'll bring you something warm to eat when you're ready."

Tony turned and left the room. He closed the door and went across the hall to his room. In his dresser, he found a pair of flannel pajamas that he never worn. He took a robe from his closet. As he started to take them across the hall, he wondered if he was doing the right thing. Maybe, it was not such a good idea to bring a complete stranger into his house. He should have taken her to the hospital, but it's too late now, he thought.

As soon as Tony had left the room, Marcie went into the bathroom. She reached into the shower and turned on the water. As soon as the water was warm, she dropped the car blanket on the floor. It was difficult for her to get undressed as she was still shaking, but she managed to get out of her raincoat and dress.

Marcie could feel the warmth of the shower slowly fill the bathroom. It seemed to help her feel better. She was able to get out of the rest of her clothes. Still shaking, she stepped into the shower. The warm water running over her cold skin caused her skin to tingle and feel prickly. It was even a little painful at first, but became tolerable fairly quickly.

Little by little, the warmth of the water warmed her body. Her shaking gradually slowed until it stopped and she was able to regain control of herself. Now that she was not so cold, she was able to wash herself. It felt good to be clean and warm again. She took her time rinsing off as the warm water felt so good on her skin.

Reluctantly, Marcie shut off the water and stepped out of the shower. She took one of the big bath towels off the rack and wrapped it around her body and dried herself. Bundled up in the big towel, she opened the door and peeked into the bedroom. There was no one in the room, but lying on the foot of the bed was a pair of men's pajamas.

She quickly realized he had brought them into the room while she was in the shower. Placing the towel over a chair, she stepped into the pajama bottoms and tied them at the waist. She then slipped into the pajama top and buttoned it up.

She was feeling very tired, but at least she was warm. The bed looked so inviting that she could not resist its calling. She pulled the covers back and crawled into the bed. Pulling the covers up, she tucked them in around her shoulders. The bed was firm, yet comfortable. The sheets and pillowcases smelled clean and fresh. It reminded her of home. She closed her eyes as she tried to remember better days.

Marcie was startled by a soft knock on the bedroom door. She turned and looked toward the door.

"Yes?" she asked softly.

"Are you decent? May I come in?"

"Yes," she replied a little reluctantly.

Marcie clutched the covers tightly around her as the door opened. She was not sure that coming here had been such a good idea. After all, she did not know this man. For all she knew, he could be a psychopathic killer. Yet, he had helped her when he could have just left her to die all alone in the parking lot. Up until now, he had done nothing that should make her feel afraid of him.

Marcie watched him as he backed into the bedroom. When he turned around, she saw that he was carrying a bed tray with a bowl of steaming hot soup on it. She looked up at him as he approached the bed.

"I thought a bowl of soup and some coffee might taste good about now. I don't know how you like your coffee, so I brought milk and sugar, just in case," he said with a smile.

Marcie noticed that he had a very pleasant smile. He hadn't asked her a bunch of questions, not even her name. He seemed to be only interested in helping her and nothing more. However, she was sure he would get to the questions sooner or later.

"Thank you," she said softly.

"I hope you feel better after your shower?" he said with a smile.

"Yes. Thank you."

She sat up in the bed, propping a pillow behind her back. Tony placed the bed tray across her lap, then stepped back and looked at her. She seemed to look much better, at least she was not shaking any more and she could talk to him.

"Is there anyone you would like to call? I wouldn't want anyone to worry unnecessarily."

Marcie looked up at him. There was someone she would like to call. She would like to call her mother and tell her that she wanted to come home, but she couldn't do it now. The idea of calling her mother sounded a little childish to her.

"No, no one," she replied, then took a sip of coffee.

Tony got the feeling that she did not feel like talking right now. He still was not sure he had done the right thing by bringing her into his home, but what else could he do? He could not have left her in the parking lot to die.

"I'll leave you alone for now. When you get finished with the soup just set the tray on the floor. I'll come get it later," he said as he turned to leave.

"Thank you."

He stopped and turned to look at her. This had been his first opportunity to really look at her. Tony had not really noticed just how pretty she was until now. The look in her eyes told him that she was indeed grateful for his help.

"You're quite welcome."

Tony gave her a big smile, then turned and left the bedroom. He returned to the kitchen and fixed himself something to eat while he tried reading the paper. His mind kept wandering to the woman in his guest room. Who was she? What was she doing in the parking lot? These questions kept him from concentrating on his paper.

While Marcie ate the soup, she could not get this man out of her mind. Somehow, he seemed to be different from most of the men she had met. He did not seem to want anything from her, only to help her. He didn't seem to be pushing for information, just accepted things the way they appeared. She almost wished she had met someone like him a long time ago. If she had, maybe her life would not be such a mess now.

Marcie finished the soup and coffee. It had warmed her inside just as the shower had warmed her outside. She set the bed tray on the floor. Scooting down in the bed, she pulled the covers up over her shoulders. The bed was warm and comfortable. She did not know why, but she felt safe and secure here. She closed her eyes, and in a very short time she was sound asleep.

CHAPTER TWO

There was a scraping sound, a sound that penetrated Marcie's mind and woke her from one of the most peaceful sleeps she had had in a very long time. Yet, the sound that had disturbed her rest did not seem to be all that strange to her. It was a sound she was sure she had heard before, but could not place at the moment.

Marcie opened her eyes and looked around the room. She felt rested for the first time in what seemed like years. Setting up in the bed, she listened. The strange sound seemed to be coming from outside, from somewhere in front of the house.

It didn't take long before curiosity finally got the best of her. She could not stand to lay there and not know what the sound was. Pushing back the comforter, she swung her feet out of the bed. Sitting up on the edge of the bed, she reached down to the foot of the bed and picked up the robe. As she stood up, she slipped her arms into the robe and wrapped it around herself. The carpet was thick and plush, and felt good under her bare feet.

She stepped up to the window and carefully pushed the curtains back so she could look outside. It was still overcast, but it had stopped snowing, at least for the moment. The first thing she noticed was a narrow balcony just outside the window. It was covered with several inches of fresh clean snow. She looked down toward the sidewalk and saw a man shoveling the snow from the sidewalk. It was the same man who had helped her last night. She smiled to herself as she realized that the strange sound she had heard was his snow shovel scraping on the concrete sidewalk as he cleared away the snow.

She took a minute to look across the street at the park. The snow clung to the trees giving them an almost stately look. The ground was covered with a clean, fresh blanket of snow. Even the street was white with only a few tracks to disturb the smooth finish of the street where cars had gone past the house.

Her eyes returned to watch the man as he worked. He was wearing a dark blue parka with a hood, but he didn't have the hood up over his head. She could see he was a handsome man with dark brown wavy hair and a strong built. He shoveled the snow off the walk with ease giving the impression that it was light and fluffy.

She guessed he was in his late twenties, maybe early thirties, but that was just the surface. She knew that much about him from what she could remember of last night. What she really wondered was, who was he and just what kind of a man was he?

One question that quickly came to her mind was, is he married? She wondered about that for a few seconds as she watched him. It hardly seemed likely he would have brought her, a woman, to his house if he were married. But then again, maybe his wife is out of town, she thought.

Her thoughts of him were interrupted when he swung the shovel over his shoulder and started back toward the porch. She took a quick look up and down the sidewalk and saw that he had finished clearing the snow away from in front of the house.

Marcie let the curtain fall back over the window and turned away. She looked around the room again, only this time noticing what was in the room. Suddenly, she caught the reflection of herself in a full-length mirror that was standing in the corner of the room. Her reflection startled her. She had never seen herself looking like this before.

Her hair was a mess, with strands of it going in all directions. She had no makeup on at all, not even a little lipstick. The robe she was wearing was several sizes too big for her, and it hung on her like a large loose gunnysack. Her feet were covered by the pajama bottoms which were much too long and dragged on the floor when she walked. She felt as if she looked like she had been on a weeklong binge.

Marcie ran her fingers through her hair as she examined her appearance in the mirror. Her appearance reminded her of the baggy clothes that were often worn by bag ladies in the street.

She became conscious of the fact that she had no comb, no lipstick, nothing that she could use to make herself presentable to this man who had been so good to her. When she had walked out of the arena, she had completely left her other life behind. She had left everything behind including her purse.

Marcie turned way from the mirror as she tried to think. She began to realize she had other problems that were far more important then how she looked. How was she going to explain to this man why she had been in the parking lot? How was she going to make him understand why she needed to get away from the lights and the crowds? He would certainly ask such questions, she thought.

It was then that another question came to mind. Did he even know who she was? She thought very hard about that question. If he did not know who she was, then she would not have to explain near as much to him. She could be anyone she wanted to be, and he would not know the difference. If he did not know who she was, then maybe, she could stay here for a few days.

A few days was all she thought she would need to get things worked out in her head. It was unlikely she would be found here, unless he already knew who she was and had called her manager or the police. If she could stay here for a couple of days, that would give her time to figure out what she needed to do. It would give her some time without the pressures of everyone trying to tell her what to do. Time to think without everyone trying to convince her to do something she really didn't want to do. It was time to decide for herself just what it was that she wanted and what was important to her.

The picture of herself in the mirror came back to mind. She slowly turned back toward the mirror to take another look at herself. If she combed her hair differently from her usual style, dressed in something far more casual than usual, she might get away with being just plain Mary Robertson, instead of the well known country singer, Marcie Roberts.

She did her best to straighten out her hair and get it looking at least a little presentable without a comb. She went into the bathroom to see what kind of condition her dress was in only to discover that all her clothes were gone. It gave her a bit of a scare and a feeling of being trapped until she remembered that he had told her to leave her clothes in the bathroom. He must have come in and taken them somewhere else to dry, she concluded.

She thought about it for a minute and decided he certainly would not recognize her in what she was wearing now, no one would. If she did not want to stay in this room forever, she would have to face him sooner or later. Now was as good a time as any.

Marcie really had no reason to trust this man, but then, she had no reason not to trust him, either. After all, he had not harmed her so far. He had done everything he could to make her as comfortable as possible. Besides she was not a prisoner, the door was not locked, or was it?

She looked across the room at the door. Her mind began to fill with all sorts of horrible thoughts. Maybe she was a prisoner. She pulled the robe tightly around her narrow waist. In doing so, she drew on all the courage she could muster. She snugged up the belt on the robe and started toward the bedroom door. Marcie looked at the doorknob for a few seconds before she reached out and put her hand on it. She then tried turning it. The knob turned easily and the door opened with hardly a sound. A soft smile came over her face as she thought about how foolish her fears had been.

Marcie looked out into the hall before venturing out of the room. There was no one in the hall and it was quiet. She started down the hall toward the stairway when she first smelled freshly brewed coffee. She suddenly realized she was hungry and remembered she had not had dinner last night, except for the cup of coffee and a bowl of soup that she had been given to warm her.

Going down the stairs and around the corner, she found herself standing in the doorway to the kitchen, not ten feet from the man. He was sitting at the table reading the morning paper.

"Good morning," he said as he looked up over his paper at her. "Are you hungry?"

His smile was pleasant. His voice was pleasing.

"Good morning, and yes." she replied softly.

He put his paper down on the table and stood up. He motioned for her to sit down.

"What would you like? I have eggs, bacon and toast, or I can fix you some oatmeal, if you like."

"Oatmeal would be fine. I haven't had hot oatmeal for years," she replied as she watched every move he made.

"Good. Oatmeal it is," he replied with a smile as he turned around and reached for the cupboard.

Marcie moved toward the table as she watched him open a cupboard and take out a box of oatmeal. She pulled out a chair and sat down at the opposite end of the table from where he had been sitting. Watching him, it was impossible for her not to notice his broad shoulders and narrow waist.

"Would you like a glass of orange juice? I'm sorry, but that is the only kind of juice I have," he said as he turned to look at her.

"Orange juice would be fine."

"I guess I'm not very well prepared for guests."

"Could I have a cup of coffee, please? It really smells good."

"Sure."

He stopped what he was doing and poured her a cup of coffee. He set it on the table in front of her, then poured her a glass of juice. He returned to the stove to finish preparing the oatmeal.

"I'm sorry I don't have something nicer for you to wear. I don't usually have women visitors," he said without turning to face her.

She wondered why he did not have women visitors. He was handsome, polite and seemed to be very nice. The house was clean and well furnished. She could see no reason why someone like him would not invite a woman to come here. Maybe, there was another reason, one that could not easily be seen.

She found it difficult not to watch his every move. There was something strange about this man. For one thing, he had not even asked her name. In fact, he had not asked her one single question except for asking her what she wanted to eat. To her that made him strange. People were always asking her personal questions, questions that she would never think of asking a stranger.

"I hope you don't mind, but I came in your room early this morning and picked up your things. I took them to the local cleaners. I'm afraid your dress might be ruined," he said as he stepped close to the table and set the bowl of oatmeal down in front of her.

Marcie just looked at him as he sat down across from her. She did not know what to say. If he had really taken her clothes to the cleaners, then she had nothing to wear, nothing at all. She suddenly felt trapped. She could feel the anxiety build in her as her heart pounded.

He noticed the look on her face. Behind those beautiful blue eyes, he thought he noticed a hint of fear. He was not sure what to do about it, but he felt he had to try. He quickly realized that she was probably feeling like a prisoner without her own clothes.

"I'm sorry," he said apologetically. "I should have waited for you to get up. I should have asked you if you wanted me to take your clothes to the cleaners. I'm sorry."

Marcie looked at him, but she did not know what to say. The look on his face seemed to tell her that he was truly sincere, that he had only meant to be helpful.

"Ah, that's all right," she said quietly.

She looked down at the bowl in front of her and watched the steam rise from the hot cereal. There was nothing she could do about it now, and she was hungry. She picked up the spoon from the sugar bowl and sprinkled sugar over the oatmeal. She then poured a little cream on the cereal and began to eat.

"I don't want to interfere in your life, but I would like to know your name?" he asked.

She stopped and looked across the table at him. Here it comes, the questions, she thought. Yet, he was simply looking at her and waiting for her reply. She hesitated.

"Okay. If you don't want to tell your name, that's all right. My name is Anthony

Beckman, Tony to my friends. You may call me Tony, if you like," he said with a smile.

When she did not reply, Tony went back to drinking his coffee and reading a little of the paper while he waited for her to finish her breakfast.

It was difficult for him to concentrate on the paper. The fact that she seemed so frightened that she would not tell him her name, caused him to wonder about her. Maybe she cannot remember her name, he thought, but that did not seem likely.

When she was finished with her juice and oatmeal, he stood up and began clearing the table. She watched him as he rinsed out the bowls and glasses and put them into the dishwasher. He had his back to her as he put the sugar bowl back in the cupboard.

"My name's Mary Robertson," she said suddenly.

Tony stopped, slowly turned, looked over his shoulder at her and smiled. "Nice to meet you, Mary Robertson."

She smiled back at him, but her smile soon faded. The way he looked at her made her feel a little self-conscious. The fact that she was wearing his robe and his pajamas, and was in his house, did not help matters any. She wished she had at least a comb and something else to wear.

Tony sensed she was feeling a little uncomfortable. He wondered if she might feel a little better if she had something else to wear, but he had taken her clothes to the cleaners. He thought about it for a minute and decided she needed something a little more practical to wear than the dress and the light raincoat he had found her in. She needed something more suitable for the winter weather in Denver, certainly more suitable than his pajamas and robe.

He returned to the table, sat down across the table and looked at her. Tony tried to pick his words very carefully. He had no desire to frighten her any more than she was already.

"Ah, I need to go out for a little while. It would be my guess that you might like me to pick up a few things for you?"

"Thank you, that would be nice. I could really use a comb and tooth brush," she said softly.

Marcie would have liked to have added a list of clothes and lipstick, but decided not to ask too much of him. She was grateful that he was willing to get her just a couple of basic things.

"Ah, I'm not sure how to say this, but would you be too offended if I picked up, say, a pair of jeans and a sweat shirt, something like that? I don't think you would really want to go outside in that outfit."

Marcie took a brief look at herself, then looked up at him. She could not keep from smiling. It was impossible for her to visualize herself out in public in his robe and pajamas.

"That would be very nice. Thank you, but I can't repay you right now."

"Well, I guess I'll just have to trust you for it. I'll be back shortly. Please, feel free to make yourself at home."

Tony stood up and walked to the coat closet next to the front door. He opened it and took out his ski jacket. Marcie watched his every move. There was something about this man that sparked her interest, something that made her want to know him better. She could not put her finger on it, but he fascinated her. Marcie could not remember ever having feelings like this about any man before. Feelings she could not describe, not even to herself.

Tony walked to the door and put his hand on the doorknob. He then stopped, turned and looked back at her. He wondered if she would be here when he got back, but where would she go? She didn't have anything to wear. He smiled more to himself than to her.

"If you need to call someone, feel free to use the phone."

"Thank you."

"Will you be all right?" he asked.

"Yes. I'll be just fine," she replied with a smile.

He nodded, then turned and walked out the door. Once he was outside, he went to his car and started it, but waited. He wondered about this woman in his house. Was Mary Robertson her real name? She seemed to be reasonably well educated, intelligent and certainly had a pleasant personality. She was certainly very pretty, but she did not fit the image he had of a street person.

Nothing seemed to add up. Maybe she was running away from something, or someone. That thought seemed more logical to him, but it still left him wondering. He shook his head, put the car in gear and pulled away from the curb.

Marcie had walked across the living room to the sofa by the window. She had watched Tony as he sat in the car. She wondered what he was thinking about as he sat there. When he finally drove off, she sat down on the sofa and looked out across the street toward the park.

She watched several children playing in the park. A couple of little girls were making snow angels in the fresh snow, while a couple of boys were throwing snowballs at the trees.

Marcie watched them as she thought of the winters back in Ohio when she was a little girl. She wondered if she would have had a little girl by now if she had married her high school sweetheart, instead of making music her life. She had always liked children and was sure she would have children of her own, someday.

The more she thought about the different directions her life could have taken, the more confused she became about what she really wanted. Even with all the confusion, the one thing she did seem to understand was that she was going to have to figure out what was most important to her and what it was that she wanted out of her life. Then she could start making plans to change her life.

She knew she did not want to keep doing what she had been doing. Going from one town to another, never stopping long enough to really meet anyone different was not the life she wanted. She did not want someone else running her life for her, telling her what to do, when to do it and where to do it.

Most of all, she did not want people taking advantage of her, using her and pushing her just so they could make more money. Sure, she made more money with the more concerts she did, but she had more than enough money to satisfy her needs. It was the greed of the others who got a cut that kept pushing her to do more, and her promoter was the worst of the bunch.

She had liked being in the spotlight at first, but now it was work, hard work. She didn't mind the hard work, but the fun and the excitement that had been there in the beginning was gone. She wanted more than just work out of her life.

She turned around and lay down on the sofa. Closing her eyes, she began to think of home. She remembered the evenings when her family would sit around the kitchen table and talk about their day, each one taking their turn. She remembered her friends coming over and talking about those important things, like who they hoped would ask them to the dance, and what they would wear.

It was an easier time back then, she thought. Why does life have to get so complicated? she asked herself. Why couldn't things be that simple again?

Tears came to her eyes. Thinking of the past was depressing for her. She had made some decisions and signed some contracts she wished she had not signed.

"If I had known then what I know now, I would not have signed my life away," she said out loud to herself.

She realized it was too late to worry about what she should have done. It was time to think about how she could make things right again. She wiped the tears from her face and sat up. This was not the time to cry, but a time to think of how she could get her life turned back around.

The first thing she understood was she would need a good lawyer. She had an attorney when she signed her contract, and it would take an attorney to get her out of the contract. That was very clear to her, but where could she find an attorney she could trust. The one she had when she signed the contract had not done a very good job of looking out for her best interests. He had made it so her contract gave almost all the rights to the promoter, which resulted in more one night shows rather than less.

It was clear she would need some help from someone, but who? She had not grown close to anyone on the tour that she felt she could talk to in confidence. If she made contact with anyone from the tour to help her, they would probably tell the promoter where she was. She did not want that to happen until she had found someone who was ready to fight for her interests.

She needed someone who was not involved with the tour or her promoter or her lawyer. She needed someone who would have nothing to gain by reporting her whereabouts. Someone who could help her find an attorney who would look out for her interests, not the interests of her promoter. She needed someone she could trust.

CHAPTER THREE

It was the sound of a car door slamming shut out in front of the house that woke Marcie with a start. She had not planned to doze off while waiting for Tony to return, but she had. Wiping her eyes, she sat up and looked out the window. Tony was coming toward the house with his arms full of packages wrapped in Christmas paper with pretty bows on them. What had he done, she wondered as she watched him walk up to the house? He told her he was going out for "a few things," but this did not look like "a few things" to her. It looked more like he had bought out the entire store.

She wondered why this man was being so nice to her. What was his motive? Why was he going way out of his way to help her, to make sure she had the things she needed? She could not remember ever being treated like this before. In the past, if anyone did something for her, it was either their job or they expected something in return. She knew it was a cynical way to look at the world, but that was how it had been for her. There was never something for nothing in her business.

She stood up, went to the door and opened it for him. She stepped back and held the door as he moved passed her.

"Thank you," he said, his arms piled so high with packages that he could barely see over them.

Marcie closed the door as she watched him deposit the packages on the sofa. She could not believe that all these things were for her. Some of them must be for him, she thought. After all, he had said that he needed to go out for some things.

He smiled at her as she looked at him with surprise. The look on her face reminded him of a little girl who had just found a big stack of Christmas packages under the tree. Yet, there was also a hint of reservation in her eyes.

"I know it's a little early for Christmas, but I didn't think you'd want to wear those things until Christmas," he said with a grin as he pointed toward her and the oversize robe she was wearing.

She looked from the packages to Tony, then back to the packages. Had he really bought all these things for her? She hesitated as she looked at the packages.

"Well. Are you going to open them? I sure hope they fit."

She looked at him once again, not sure if she should accept his gifts or not. He was smiling at her, and the gleam in his eyes told her that he was enjoying this. He was like a little kid who had managed to keep a big surprise a secret.

"Are all these for me?"

"They sure are. I hope you don't mind. I think your dress is ruined, and you don't have anything else to wear."

She looked back at the packages. "I won't be able to pay you back for awhile."

"I didn't ask to be paid back. These things are yours with no strings attached. I want nothing in return, nor do I want you to pay me back for them. You owe me nothing," he countered more sharply than he had intended.

The tone in his voice told her that she might have hurt his feelings. He had bought them as gifts for her, and that was all. He said that he neither wanted, nor expected anything in return. If that was truly the case, then this man was different all right. He was giving her things she wanted and needed, and did not put a price on them. It had been a long time since she had met someone like him.

She was feeling a little guilty about hurting his feelings, but she could not help herself. It was hard for her to accept a gift without thinking that there would be some kind of pay back required. She had known so few people who didn't want something in return for anything they did for her, no matter how small it might be. This was no small thing he had done for her.

"I'm sorry. I really do appreciate them."

Tony did not respond other than to simply nod his head. He had accepted her apology, but he wondered why she was afraid that everything had some hidden meaning to it. What kind of a life had she been living to become so cynical at such a young age?

Marcie moved over to the sofa and started to open the packages. As he stood by and watched her take each item out of its package, he noticed how her face lit up. She neatly stacked up the clothes in a pile after unwrapping and looking at each of them.

Tony noticed that she appeared to be a neat person, very well organized. She even folded the wrappings and stacked them neatly next to the clothes.

When she was finished, she turned around to look up at Tony. He was standing only a few feet from her. As she looked into his eyes, she stepped in front of him. She reached out and touched his cheek. Rising up on her tiptoes, she kissed him lightly on the lips, then stepped back.

"Thank you, thank you very much," she said in almost a whisper.

"You're very welcome," he replied looking down at her.

Her light kiss had been warm and gentle, and her fingers touching his cheek had been as light as a feather. Neither of them spoke for several seconds. They just looked at each other. He wanted to take her in his arms, but decided that to do so might well reinforce her fear that he wanted something from her in return for the gifts. Tony was the first to break the silence.

"Are you going to try them on?"

"Oh, yes. I guess that would be a good idea," she replied sheepishly.

"I hope everything fits. If it doesn't, I'll take them back and get the right sizes."

"I'm sure the jeans will fit. The legs might be a little long, but other than that they are the right size. And the sweatshirts will be fine."

"There's a comb and toothbrush in the small bag over there." he said as he pointed at a paper bag near the end of the sofa.

"I wasn't sure what else you would need," he added.

"Thank you very much. I'll go change."

She gathered up all the things he had bought for her and started for the stairs. Just as she turned to go up the stairs, Tony called to her.

"Would you like me to make some coffee?"

She stopped, turned toward him and smiled. It was hard for her to remember the last time she had met anyone who had been so concerned about her and what she wanted. Even something as simple as offering her a cup of coffee made her feel good.

"That would be nice," she replied with a smile.

"I'll have it ready when you come down," he said with a smile.

"Thank you."

She then turned and went on upstairs.

Tony watched her as she carried her new clothes upstairs. As soon as she was out of sight, he went into the kitchen and made a pot of coffee.

Marcie entered her bedroom and set the clothes down on the bed. As she laid out the clothes, she realized that he had bought her three changes of clothes. There were two pair of jeans and a pair of slacks, two very nice colorful sweatshirts and a flowered blouse that would go very nicely with the slacks.

There was a pair of snow boots, a pair of tennis shoes and three pair of cotton socks.

She smiled to herself when she realized he had not gotten her any panties or bras. Considering everything, he had done very well. She might have been a little concerned about him if he had gotten those items for her. Besides, he did not know what size she would need. As it was, he had guessed pretty well on the sizes of what he did get for her. Except of the length of the jeans, she was pretty sure everything would fit. She would just have to go without underwear until they could go out again.

Marcie took off the robe and hung it on a hook on the back of the bathroom door. She decided that jeans and a sweatshirt with tennis shoes would be a good choice for now. If she simply rolled up the pant legs a turn or two they would be fine.

She sat down on the bed and removed the tags from the clothes. When she was finished, she picked the pink sweatshirt with little birds on it to wear with jeans.

She unbuttoned the pajama top and slipped out of it, then slipped out of the bottoms. She had not realized how cool it was in her bedroom until she was standing there without a stitch on. She quickly picked up the jeans and stepped into them, pulling them up over her shapely legs and hips. She quickly pulled the zipper up and buttoned the waistband. The jeans fit her well, except for the length.

Marcie picked up the sweatshirt, slid her arms into the sleeves and raised it up over her head. She pulled the shirt down over her firm smooth breasts and down past her narrow waist. The soft flannel inside of the sweatshirt felt good on her bare skin. She immediately felt warmer. Sitting down on the edge of the bed, she rolled up her pant legs a couple of inches, then put on a pair of sox and the tennis shoes. She was a little surprised to find that the shoes fit her perfectly.

Marcie took the comb and toothbrush from the small bag and went into the bathroom. After brushing her teeth, she began to see what she could do with her hair. It soon became apparent that she was going to have to simply put it up in sort of a ponytail for now. She decided she could fix it later, after she washed it.

She combed out her hair. Her shoulder length blond hair was shiny and soft. As she combed it, she gathered it into a ponytail, but realized she did not have anything to tie it. Since she was dressed, she held her hair in the ponytail and went back downstairs.

"Do you have a ribbon or a rubber band? Something I could use to tie my hair back?"

Tony looked up from his paper and saw her standing in the doorway. She was beautiful. Her hair was long and a very unusual yellow blond. It seemed to sparkle in the light. Her eyes were the most beautiful blue he had ever seen. Her skin looked smooth like fine porcelain, only it looked soft, too.

"Ah, yeah. I think I can find you a rubber band in my desk."

He stood up and walked past her. She followed him to his desk and watched him as he opened one of the desk drawers. He picked up a rubber band and held it out to her.

"Will this do?"

"Yes. That will do just fine."

She took the rubber band and began tying her ponytail with it. When she was finished, she smiled at him.

"How's that look?"

"Very nice. Oh, by the way, I did get you a jacket that is a little more suitable for the weather here in Denver. I thought we could go out after lunch and get anything else you might need," he said shyly.

"Like, maybe, some underwear?" she asked.

"Yeah," he answered with a shy sort of smile.

She smiled at him. It was easy to see that it was at least a little embarrassing for him to talk about women's underwear, especially since he did not know her.

"We should be able to get your things from the cleaners this afternoon. Coffee's ready."

"Great," she replied with a smile.

Marcie followed Tony back to the kitchen table. She sat down while Tony poured them each a cup. As she watched him, she wondered if he had ever been married. Something about the way he acted made her pretty sure he was not married now, but may have been married at one time. She had had time to look around a little. The way the house was decorated indicated a woman had at least helped him with the decorating. It had a woman's touch.

"You have a very lovely house here. Did you decorate it yourself?

"Ah, no, not really. I had a friend help me with it."

"A female friend?"

"As a matter of fact, yes."

"She has good taste."

Since Tony did not respond further, she wondered if she was getting into an area that he would rather keep private, after all she was a stranger to him. She decided it might be best if she changed the subject.

"Do you often get snow like this?"

"Yes. We sometimes get more. This is pretty typical weather for this time of year."

It was apparent to Tony that she was not from around here, or she would know this was typical weather for December. He had a dozen or more questions to ask her, but did not want to pry into her affairs. On the other hand, she had asked him some rather personal questions, and turn about was fair play.

"Where are you from, originally, I mean?"

She looked across the table at him and hesitated. Now he was going to want to know all about her. She wished she had not started asking questions.

"I'm from back east."

In giving him such a vague answer, she hoped he would not pursue it any further. She wanted to trust him, but was still afraid to trust him with too much of her life. She needed a friend right about now, but she was not secure enough with him, not yet.

"Where back east?" he asked as he sipped his coffee.

Marcie quickly decided to continue to be Mary Robertson for a few days. If she told him a little about Mary Robertson and nothing about Marcie Roberts, she would not be tripped up in a lie.

"I'm from a little town in southern Ohio. I'm from Mulberry, Ohio."

"Just where is Mulberry, Ohio?" he asked with a grin.

"It's near Cincinnati."

After she told him were she was from, she wished she had chosen a different town. She realized if the newspapers found out she was missing, they might also report that she was originally from Mulberry, Ohio. With Mulberry being such a small town, she was sure he would be able to put it together and know she was Marcie Roberts, the country singer. Especially, since he had found her not far from the arena where Marcie Roberts was to perform.

She knew it was too late now. If he figured it out, she would have to try to explain things to him. Right now, she would continue to be Mary Robertson, and that was who she wanted to be for as long as possible. She thought it was probably a good time to change the subject.

"I take it you were at the football game last night. Did your team win?"

"Not this time, but they do have a winning record this year. I really don't follow football very much."

"Then why were you at the game if you don't follow the sport?" she asked a little confused.

"One of my friends gave me a couple of tickets to the game. I didn't have anything else to do, so I went."

"You said that you had a "couple of tickets." Did you take someone with you?"

"Well, yes and no. I met my friend at the game, but she had to leave just after half time. I decided to stay to the end."

"I'm glad you stayed."

Tony looked into her bright blue eyes. He was glad he had stayed, too. He was not sure if she was glad because he had saved her life, or because she was here with him now.

"Was your 'friend' the one who helped you decorate your house?"

"Yes. Yes, she was."

Marcie was not sure how she felt about his answer. She felt a twinge of something, but she was not sure what it could be. She quickly rejected her thought that it may have been a twinge of jealousy. After all, why should she be jealous of another woman when it came to this man. She hardly knew him.

"Is she your main squeeze, your woman?"

Tony was not sure how to answer her. He wasn't sure he wanted to answer her. 'Your woman' as Mary put it, was the woman he had been dating for some time. In fact, she was the only woman he had dated since his divorce over three years ago.

"I guess you could say that."

Marcie felt that same twinge again. She began to think that maybe it was not such a good idea to stay here. She did not want to come between him and his woman, but if she didn't stay here, where would she go?

"How about some lunch," Tony said in an effort to change the subject.

"Sounds like a good idea," she replied, glad that he had changed the subject.

Marcie was sure that if she had her mouth full of food, it would be more difficult for her to put her foot in it. She had been treading on some very private ground, and his love life was really none of her business.

"Is there anything I can do to help?"

"No. You are my guest, besides there isn't much to choose from. It looks like sandwiches are what you will get."

"That would be fine with me."

Tony stood up and went to the refrigerator. He gathered up some lunchmeat and cheese, a bottle of dressing and a carton of milk. After setting them on the table, he went to the cupboard for a loaf of bread. As soon as the table was set and Tony had sat down, they each began fixing their own sandwiches. They did very little talking during lunch. It seemed that neither of them was willing to talk very much about themselves.

After lunch, she helped him clear the table and put things away. Being in the kitchen with him seemed as natural to her as being at home. She liked the feeling of being close to him, even if she hardly knew him.

"Why don't you get your boots on, and we will go to the mall for those other things you need?"

She smiled at what he had said then replied, "Okay."

Marcie went upstairs and within a few minutes she returned to the living room. Tony was standing near the front door holding a blue ski jacket with a matching scarf.

"Is that for me?"

"Yes. You can't very well go outside without one. It's cold out there."

"Yes, I know," she said as she remembered last night and how cold it had been.

He held it out for her. She moved up in front of him and turned around. He helped her as she slipped her arms into the sleeves. As she turned around, he stepped closer to her and wrapped the scarf around her neck. Looking up at him, she could feel her heart pound. He was so close she could feel his breath against her hair.

Slowly, he put his hands on her shoulders and gently pulled her to him. She put her hands on his waist as she tipped her head back to look up at him. He was going to kiss her, she was sure of it. She wanted him to kiss her. It had been so long since she had been held by anyone who cared about her. It had been even longer since anyone had kissed her.

Suddenly, the spell was broken by the harsh sound of the telephone ringing. She could not remember when a telephone had sounded so loud or so irritating. Tony looked off toward the phone as he let out a discussed sigh, then looked back at Mary.

"Excuse me, please."

It was clear that Tony was not happy with the phone ringing when it did. A few minutes earlier, or a few minutes later, would have suited him just fine. Marcie was sure that she would have preferred later, much later.

She stayed near the door while Tony walked across the room to answer the phone. She watched him as he picked up the receiver. He was looking at her when he put the receiver to his ear, but quickly turned his back to her when he realized who was calling. From the way he acted, Marcie was convinced that the person on the other end of the phone was most likely his girlfriend. She could not hear what was being said, but she sensed that Tony was trying to either get out of a date, or get off the phone.

Marcie was beginning to feel that she was interfering in his life. She did not want to interfere in his life. It was hard for her not to think of him and his feelings. She wanted to leave, right now, before she caused him any problems with his girlfriend. Yet, she wanted to stay and be near him. She liked him, and not because he had saved her life or because he had bought her clothes. He seemed to be everything she had wanted in a man, a man she could love.

The thought that she might be falling in love with him was very unsettling for her. Falling in love with any man right now would only make things more complicated for her. She certainly did not want to make her life any more complicated than it was already. She had all the complications she could handle, and then some.

Tony hung up the phone. He turned and looked at her. It took a few seconds before he could manage to force a smile.

"Well, are you ready to go?"

"Sure, but if you have other things you need to take care of, we could go some other time," she said as she looked up at him.

Tony moved to the door, opened the door and held it for her.

"Everything's fine," he assured her.

Marcie forced a smile and walked by him. He stepped out on the porch, closed the door and locked it. Together they walked to the curb where he held the car door for her. As soon as she was in the car, he closed the door, went around to the other side and got in. He started the car and pulled away from the curb.

CHAPTER FOUR

The clouds still hung low over the mile high city. There was little possibility that the sky would clear and the sun would come out today. In fact, it looked like it might snow again at any moment. Most of the side streets were slippery from the hard packed snow, while many of the main streets were wet from the salt and sand that had been spread on them by the city trucks. The temperature was well below freezing and there was a cold, sharp wind blowing down off the mountains.

One thing Marcie had noticed was how fast some of the people were driving, even with the icy intersections. She was afraid someone might run into them.

The drive to the mall was one of silence. Neither of them had very much to say. They were each lost in their own thoughts. Marcie found herself glancing in his direction on several occasions while he drove.

As Tony turned into the mall parking lot, Marcie wondered if she might be recognized by one of her many fans. After giving it some thought, she was pretty sure no one would recognize her with her hair in a ponytail and without any makeup.

She also wondered what Tony was thinking about. He seemed to be preoccupied ever since the phone call. Marcie was sure it had been his girlfriend who had called.

Tony was thinking about the phone call. It had been Linda Forrest, a lawyer who worked for a large law firm based in Denver. He had been dating Linda for the past couple of years. Everyone was convinced that the two of them would eventually get married.

Tony had been reluctant to make any kind of commitment. He had been burned very badly in his first marriage to a woman who was domineering, demanding, and who did not trust him around other women, even women he had to work with on different projects. He had never given her any reason not to trust him. He did not want that kind of a relationship again.

He and Linda had been talking about getting married for almost a year. Actually, it was Linda who had been doing all the talking. Last night at the football game, he had come very close to telling Linda that he would marry her, but for some unknown reason he had decided to wait for a better time and place.

It sounded funny when he thought about it. It sounded like it was Linda who was asking him to marry her. The more he thought about it, the more he realized it had been her idea all along, not his. He had been the one dragging his feet. He was the one who had been reluctant to take the plunge. He did not even like to talk about marriage.

Now there was another problem, the woman sitting beside him in the car. It seemed that Mary's presence had brought doubts about his relationship with Linda back into the forefront of his mind. Was marrying Linda the thing he should do? Just the fact he had to ask himself that very question, made him completely unsure of the answer. Why was he so unsure, especially now? Yesterday evening he had been sure or at least he thought he was sure. Today, he wasn't at all sure.

Was he just getting cold feet or was there some other reason?

Tony had to mentally shake himself. This stranger sitting beside him would be gone in a day or two, and that would be the end of it, he thought. She would be just one of those many people who come into your life and then disappear, never to be seen or heard from again. No matter how hard he thought about it, his doubts about Linda would not go away.

He turned into a parking place and shut off the engine. Looking at Mary, he found her fascinating, but why? What was it that made her so fascinating? She was certainly a very beautiful woman, but there was more to it than that. There was something very special about her, something mysterious. Something he could not understand, yet.

"Are we going in?" she asked as she looked at him and waited for him to get out of the car.

"Yeah."

She had caught him off guard with her question. It made him feel just a little foolish.

They got out of the car. Marcie did not wait for him to come around and open her door this time. He met her at the back of the car and then he walked beside her into the mall.

Once inside the Mall's main entrance, Marcie began looking around. The Mall was full of people. She was sure that many of them were doing their Christmas shopping. There was Christmas music coming from the ceiling, parents trying to keep track of their kids, and all kinds of Christmas decorations with their flashing colored lights everywhere.

She reached out and took hold of Tony's arm. He looked down at her and she smiled up at him. He was a little surprised she had taken his arm, but he was certainly not going to object. It seemed right for her to be on his arm.

"I remember as a small girl I got lost in a big mall like this," she said in an effort to explain her action.

"Stick with me and you won't get lost," he assured her.

"I will," she replied as she looked up at him.

Marcie gave his arm a squeeze as they wandered through the crowd. She had never been in this mall before, so she was more than willing to let him lead the way. As they passed the center court, they saw a line of kids waiting to see Santa Claus. It was easy to see the excitement in the eyes of the children. There was, however, one little boy who was crying. Apparently, the sight of this big bearded man in the bright red suit had frightened him. Marcie felt sorry for the little guy.

Marcie rarely got a chance to just walk around in a mall anymore. It seemed she never had time for that sort of thing. She was enjoying herself today, just looking around and watching the people.

Tony made a sudden turn into a woman's store. She had not expected him to turn so quickly and almost lost her hold of him. She had been too busy looking around and watching the different people. It took her a couple of steps to catch up with him.

"I think you will find everything you need in here."

"If you would feel more comfortable waiting outside, I'd understand," she said looking up at him.

"First of all, I really don't mind waiting in the store while you decide on what you want. Secondly, if I'm out there somewhere, how are you going to pay for what you want in here?"

"You have a very good point there," she conceded, realizing that she was dependent on him for the things she needed.

Marcie wished she did not need to have him pay for things for her, but that couldn't be helped right now. She would simply have to swallow her pride and promise herself that she would pay him back later. She looked around for the lingerie department. As soon as she located it, she pointed it out to Tony.

"Lead on," he said with a smile.

He followed her as she worked her way around racks stuffed with the latest styles in clothing. Many of the styles did not impress Tony very much, but they seemed to be selling.

Once they arrived in the lingerie department, Tony walked over next to the cashier's counter to wait for Marcie to pick out the things she needed. It seemed to Tony that every woman in this department was watching him. He remembered having been in the lingerie section of stores before with his wife, but he always felt a little out of place and a little uncomfortable, today was no different.

Marcie picked out the things she needed. As she came toward the cashier's counter, Tony pointed to a rack of nightgowns. She stopped and looked at the rack, then walked up to the cashier's counter. She set the items she needed on the counter.

"Don't you want to get a nightgown?" Tony asked.

"You have spent more than enough on me. I can get along without one."

"Why don't you pick one out? I'm sure you would prefer a nightgown to my pajamas," he said quietly so as not to embarrass her.

She smiled up at him. There was no question that she would prefer a nightgown to his oversize pajamas. A nightgown that fit her would be more comfortable. As she looked over the rack of nightgowns, she noticed there were three or four different styles in three or four different colors. Marcie picked out a soft long nightgown with a lacy bodice in a light mint green. She held it up in front of her and turned toward Tony for his approval.

Tony looked at the nightgown and tried to imagine her wearing it. He liked the style of the nightgown, but did not care much for the color. He shook his head in disapproval.

"Try the blue one," he suggested.

She turned around and hung the nightgown back on the rack. She picked out another one in her size of the same style, only in a light blue and held it up in front of her. Marcie could tell by the smile on Tony's face that he definitely approved of this one. She smiled back and walked up to the counter where she added it to the other items to be purchased.

"Will that be all?" the sales clerk asked.

"Yes," Marcie replied.

"Cash or charge?"

"Charge," Tony replied as he handed the sales clerk his charge card.

Marcie moved over and stood close to Tony while the sales clerk rang up the sale.

She watched him as he watched the sales clerk. She wondered what it was about this man that made her want to be near him. He was handsome, but that was a surface thing. He certainly was generous, but that was not why she wanted to be near him. After all, she had all the money she needed, just not available to her at this moment. There was something that drew her to him, but she could not figure out just what it was. Her thoughts of him were interrupted when the sales clerk handed Tony a sack with her purchases.

"You ready?" Tony asked as he looked down and smiled.

"Yes," she replied.

Tony thanked the sales clerk, then turned toward the door. Marcie walked out of the store at his side. She felt very secure with him.

"What would you like to do now?"

"Would it be all right if we just walk around the mall for a little while?"

"Sure. Any place special?"

"No. I would like to just look around."

"Okay."

Tony held out his arm and smiled at her. She looped her arm in his, and they began strolling through the mall. They took their time as if they had all the time in the world. They stopped and looked in the windows of each store they passed. As they passed a pet store, they stopped and watched a little puppy playing with a rubber ball. The puppy stopped playing and looked up at Marcie.

"Isn't he cute?"

"Yes, but I would be willing to bet he won't stay that cute."

"Maybe not, but he is adorable now."

"Do you want him?"

Marcie looked up at Tony. He had surprised her with the suggestion of getting her a dog, and it confused her. Was there some kind of hidden meaning behind what he had asked, she wondered? Getting a dog meant responsibility, time and effort to care for it.

"I don't think it would be a good idea right now."

Tony knew she was right and what she meant. He wondered how long she would be around, too. He was as surprised as she was that he had even considered buying the dog. It had just sort of slipped out. He hoped she would stay around, but was not sure why he felt that way.

"I guess you're right," he replied.

Without another word, they moved on. They walked through several other stores, looking at all the different items that were offered for sale. They seemed to especially enjoy the stores offering art items. They both seemed to like the western art best.

Just as they were coming out of an art store, they almost ran into Linda Forrest. Tony was very surprised to see her. In fact, he was so surprised that he dropped the packages. When the packages hit the floor, a small box displaying a picture of a woman in panties slid out of the bag.

Linda watched Tony as he bent over and picked up the packages. There was no doubt in Tony's mind that she had seen the box of panties and that it was going to be a very difficult thing to explain.

Linda had noticed that Marcie's arm had been looped through Tony's arm before he bent down. She looked at Marcie's face, then at Tony's. As he stood up, Marcie once again put her arm through his. Marcie did not know who this woman was and could not understand why the woman seemed so upset when she looked at them.

Linda did not know what she was looking for, but she needed to see something that would make sense to her. Something that would help her understand what Tony was doing with this woman. Linda did not know what to say either. It was a shock for her to see Tony with another woman. She had not expected to see him here at all, and especially not with a woman on his arm.

"Hi, Linda." Tony managed to get that much out as he grasped for something to say. He quickly realized that he was going to have a difficult time explaining Mary's presence to Linda. It made him feel somewhat awkward.

"Well, I didn't expect to see you here," Linda said sharply.

The tone in Linda's voice was as cold, if not colder, than the wind outside. Her comment was also an understatement.

Marcie saw the way this woman looked at Tony. It was obvious that she was very upset, and very angry with him. She could not understand why this woman was so upset, and then it hit her. This woman must be Tony's girlfriend. Marcie slipped her arm out of Tony's. She knew it was too late, the damage to Tony's and Linda's relationship was already done. Marcie felt like stepping back and slipping around behind Tony, but stayed at his side.

"I didn't expect to see you, either," Tony responded.

It was clear Tony was at a loss for words. He felt Mary take her arm away, but was glad she did not back away.

"I'll just bet," Linda replied sharply.

Tony did not like her sharp reply. He quickly became angry with her. After all, he was not married to her, nor was he even engaged to her. Linda had no right to be so rude in front of his new friend. He straightened up his shoulders and looked her right in the eyes.

"Linda, I would like you to meet a friend of mine. This is Mary Robertson. Mary, this is Linda Forrest."

Tony spoke clearly and firmly, without any hint of apology. He felt he had nothing to apologize for. There was no reason for Tony to explain anything to Linda. After all, she did not own him. He felt if they did become engaged things would be different, but at least for now, what he was doing with this woman was none of Linda's business.

Tony also could see no reason to mention to Mary that he had been going with Linda for the past couple of years. To Tony, it was not important and there was no sense making an issue out of it, especially here. He was sure Mary would probably be out of his life in a few days, anyway.

"Hi," Marcie said weakly.

It was clear to Marcie that no matter what she said to Linda, it would be the wrong thing. There was no way Linda was going to listen to any explanation from her, or anyone else for that matter. Marcie felt it would be better to just let it lie and say nothing more. If Tony wanted to try to explain why he was with her, that was up to him.

Linda looked at Mary, but did not respond. Linda was having a difficult time dealing with the rush of feelings. She was sure she was in love with Tony, at least she was before this unexpected meeting. Linda was confused and hurt seeing Tony with another woman. Not knowing just what to say or do, she simply turned sharply and walked away.

Marcie looked up at Tony. He was watching Linda as she stormed off down the mall. Marcie wondered if Tony wanted to go after her. If he did want to go after her, why didn't he? She would certainly understand.

Tony turned and looked at Mary. He felt he should try to explain what just happened, but explain what? He could see no reason for Linda to have treated Mary so rudely. Linda did not own him. It made him angry to think that Linda thought she had exclusive rights to him.

Maybe, he had just seen the real Linda for the first time and he did not like what he saw. Linda had acted too much like his first wife, and that thought scared him.

"Maybe, we should just go," Marcie suggested.

"Okay, if that's what you want, but we don't have to go."

"Please."

Tony hesitated for a second, but then started off down the mall toward the entrance. He did not hurry, but walked at a steady pace. They did not speak. He felt as if he should apologize to Mary for Linda's rudeness, but chose instead to say nothing. Instead, he reached out with his free hand and took hold of Mary's hand.

Marcie walked beside him and wondered what he was thinking. She briefly looked up at him. He was looking straight ahead. His gentle, but firm touch sent a rush through her. Somehow, just having his hand in hers made her feel better about Tony's confrontation with Linda.

They weaved their way through the crowd of people as they worked their way to the entrance. Once outside the mall, they went directly to Tony's car. He unlocked the door and held it for her as she got in. He set the packages on the rear seat, then got in himself. Soon they were heading back toward Tony's house.

Marcie wanted to tell Tony that she was sorry she had upset his girl friend, and that she had not wanted to interfere with his relationship with Linda. She just knew it was her fault that he had sharp words with Linda. What right did she have to come into someone's life and disrupt it, then leave? If it had not been for her childish attempt to escape from her own unhappy life, she would not have torn his world apart. She almost wished that she had let him take her to the hospital instead of to his home.

Feeling guilty, Marcie decided it would be best for all concerned if she just returned to her own world and left him to his. When they got back to his house, she would call her manager and tell him where she was staying.

He would come and get her, and pay Tony for all the things he had purchased for her. She would then be out of his life, forever.

Marcie looked over at Tony as he drove. She immediately began to question her own resolve. Marcie had never met a man quite like him. She liked being with him. He made her feel safe and secure. He was nice to her, and seemed to like her. Tony didn't ask much of her, yet he seemed to feel he should protect her. Marcie did not want to leave him, not yet anyway. She liked being treated like a human being for a change, not just another piece of property to be used and discarded when it was no longer of any value. Maybe, she would stay just a little while longer, she thought.

Tony's head was filled with his own thoughts. He was angry with Linda for jumping to conclusions. After all, Linda was an attorney. It only seemed fair that he should be given the same rights as a common street criminal, innocent until proven guilty. The only thing Tony felt he might be guilty of was helping someone who needed help, and it just happened to be a woman. Maybe, he had gone a little farther than would be considered normal in his effort to help her, but that was his decision to make, not hers.

Linda had no right to be rude to Mary, either. She did not even take the time to find out who this woman was, and why she was with him.

Why was he with her? What was it that drew him to want to be with her? It was obvious that she was a very beautiful woman, but that was only a part of it. What was it about this woman that captivated him so, that made him want to get to know her better?

It was this last question that filled his thoughts. She seemed to need his help, but yet he was sure that deep down this woman was as strong-willed as any woman he had ever met. He was sure that she could be gentle and loving, too. Up to now, she had made no demands of him. Yet, with all these things going for her, he sensed that she had some inner struggle going on within her. What could be this woman's trouble? How could he help her? Would she even let him help her?

Tony pulled up to the curb in front of the house and stopped the car. He shut off the engine and looked over at Marcie. He did not say anything for what seemed like a long time.

"I'm sorry about the way Linda treated you," he said.

"That's all right."

"No, it isn't. She had no right to be rude to you."

Marcie looked at him. She had come into his life, made a mess out of it and made him very unhappy. She may have even ruined his chance for a life with Linda.

"I think it would be best if I go. I have made a mess of things for you. I'm the one who should be sorry."

"You've done nothing. Let's go in and see what we can find for dinner. We can talk about your leaving later," Tony suggested.

Tony smiled at her. She liked to see him smile. There was something special about his smile. It just seemed to make her feel warm inside and make things better. She could not resist his smile.

Tony got out of the car. He walked around and opened the door for her. She got out and waited until he had gathered up the packages. Together, they walked up to the house. Once inside, she took the packages upstairs to her bedroom while he hung up their coats.

When she returned, he was sitting on the sofa watching the news. Her heart sank as she heard the newscaster talking about the disappearance of Marcie Roberts, the country western singer. She just knew Tony would see that she was really Marcie Roberts.

The picture of her on the TV screen was one that had been taken when her hair was shorter and fixed in a curly perm. She was also dressed in a very western styled outfit. It did not look much like her right now. It was a relief for her to see the news station had used an old promotional photo.

Tony looked up at her. She had a strange look on her face, as if maybe she was not feeling very well.

"Are you all right?"

Marcie turned and looked at him. It took a second for her to respond.

"Yes. Yes, I'm fine."

"Come sit with me."

Marcie could hear the concern in his voice. She moved around to the front of the sofa and sat down beside him. As soon as the news changed to a different subject, she let out a sigh of relief. She was almost sure he had not made the connection between Marcie Roberts and Mary Robertson. At least he had not given her any indication that he knew who she really was.

As soon as the news was over, Tony stood up. He looked down at her.

"You getting hungry?"

"A little."

"Tell you what, I'll fix us something to eat. Why don't you just relax."

"I can help."

"No, you just relax. After last night, you must be a little tired."

"I guess I am," she replied, giving in to his suggestion.

Tony nodded in agreement. He then turned and went out to the kitchen to fix dinner.

Marcie let out a big sigh as soon as he was gone. She knew that it would not be long before he would figure out who she was. If she was going to get things worked out and make any kind of meaningful decisions about her own future, she was going to have to find some time to think. Some place where she could be alone and not distracted by Tony.

She lay down on the sofa, curled up and closed her eyes. Marcie tried to think about her career and her future as a singer, but thoughts of Tony kept creeping in and distracting her. She even remembered how it felt to kiss him, and wondered if she was falling in love with him. She never got the chance to answer herself as she dozed off into a peaceful sleep.

CHAPTER FIVE

Tony had just finished setting the table and was ready to put the dinner on. He went into the living room to tell Marcie that dinner was ready and found her sleeping on the sofa. She looked so much at peace that he hesitated to wake her. He just stood quietly in the doorway looking at her.

Tony thought the color of her hair was rather unusual. It was blond, but its color was more of a bright yellow. Even though it was an unusual color, it was very pretty.

Her face had very delicate features and her skin appeared smooth and soft. She was not very tall, yet her build was very well proportioned to her height. While the sweatshirt sort of hid the features of her upper body, her jeans accented the smooth curved lines of her hips and legs.

There was something about this woman, something that seemed slightly familiar. He could not quite figure out what it was that made him think he had seen her before. It was possible that he had seen her somewhere around Denver, maybe at one of the many office buildings that he had been in at one time or another. He just shook his head. He could not remember where, or under what circumstances he had seen her before. He even thought of asking her, but did not want to pry into her business.

Although there was something very special about this woman, there was also something about her that worried him, too. She had to be very deeply troubled about something to have risked freezing to death to escape it. He was sure she was running away from something or someone. Why else would she have been hiding behind his car? He had not seen anyone chasing her or looking for her at the stadium, but he had not really looked.

She was definitely a mystery to him. She had no purse or any identification, at least not that he had seen. There was nothing in her coat pockets that would help identify her. She was not dressed for the weather, so he was sure that she had not gone very far before he found her. He was sure that she needed help and he wanted to help her, but she would have to ask for his help. In that way he would not be interfering in her life.

Tony was so deep in his thoughts of her that he had not realized that she was looking back at him. He had not seen her open her eyes. It embarrassed him a little getting caught watching her sleep.

"I'm sorry," he said sheepishly.

"That's okay," she replied with a smile.

"Dinner's ready."

"Okay."

Marcie got up from the sofa and walked across the room. Tony stepped aside to allow her to pass as she approached the doorway, then followed her into the dining room.

"You can sit here," he said as he pulled the chair back for her.

"Thank you," she said as she sat down and he pushed her chair up to the table.

Marcie looked over the table and noted it had been set with a great deal of care. She was a little surprised at the effort he had gone to for just a simple Saturday evening meal. There was a tablecloth on the table, very nice crystal goblets and very beautiful china. It was almost as if he were trying to impress her. She had to admit to herself that he had done a good job of it so far.

"This is very nice," she said as she smiled up at him.

"Thank you," he replied as he smiled at her, then went into the kitchen.

Marcie could smell something and it smelled very good. She wondered what he had prepared for dinner.

"Whatever it is, it sure smells good," she called out to him.

"Good, I hope you are hungry. I made enough to feed an army," he replied as he came through the kitchen door carrying a serving platter.

Tony set the platter on the table and sat down. She looked at the dish. It was strips of chicken in mixed vegetables over a bed of rice. It looked delicious. She took a deep breath as she smelled its pleasant aroma.

"Your plate, please?"

Marcie handed him her plate and watched him as he spooned some of the hot dish onto it. As soon as he had served her, he dished up some for himself. He set his plate down and waited for her to sample the meal first. She took a small portion on her fork and put it in her mouth.

"Mmmmmmm. This is delicious," she said with a smile.

It was clear by the look on Tony's face that he was pleased she liked it.

They sat silently eating dinner. Marcie could not help but notice that Tony kept looking over at her as if there was something he wanted to say, or maybe ask. She was beginning to feel a little uncomfortable. It was even making her a little nervous.

There were a lot of questions in Tony's mind. He wanted to know who this woman really was? What was she doing in the parking lot? Why was she hiding behind his car? What was she running from? Why was he so fascinated by her?

Tony paused and put his fork down. He put his elbows on the table and leaned forward. He looked into Marcie's soft blue eyes.

"I'm sorry, and I don't mean to be sticking my nose into your business, but I need to ask you something. Are you in some kind of trouble?"

Marcie looked into his eyes and hesitated. Something inside her wanted to tell him the truth, but another part of her said "no, not yet". He had done more than anyone had ever done for her before, yet she was still not sure she could trust him. She needed more time. She looked down at her plate as she could not look into his eyes any longer and lie to him.

"No," she said softly.

Tony was sure she was not telling him the truth, at least not the whole truth. He wanted her to trust him and share her problems with him. Maybe, he could be of some help. He could not help her if he didn't know what was troubling her.

"I'm sorry. It's just that you seem so worried about something, or afraid of something or someone."

She looked up at him. He was trying too hard to get close to her, and she could not let that happen, not right now. If he got too close to her, it would just complicate things even more.

"I'm not afraid of anything," she blurted out in her frustration.

She was trying very hard to show him that she was as strong as anyone was, but she didn't really feel very strong right now. Marcie wanted to ask him for his help, but she was afraid to ask. She pushed back the chair and stood up. Without a single word, she turned and quickly left the room. She ran up the stairs to the bedroom.

Tony stood up and began to follow her. His first impulse was to follow her up the stairs, but he stopped at the doorway. He quickly decided against it as he watched her disappear into her room. Tony heard the door to her room slam shut.

Suddenly, he was angry with himself for pushing her so hard. He would give her a few minutes by herself. Then, he would go up and apologize to her for butting into her business. He had no idea what was troubling her, but he had no desire to make things harder for her, either. All he wanted was to help her, if she would let him.

As soon as she had disappeared into the bedroom, he turned around and went back into the dining room. Looking at the table, he noticed she had eaten only about half of the food on her plate. He had not finished his dinner either, but he did not feel very hungry anymore. He began clearing the table, more to keep himself busy than anything else.

Marcie pushed the bedroom door closed behind her as she ran toward the bed. She flopped down on the bed and buried her face in the pillow. The pillow muffled her sobs. She could not help herself. It seemed no one would leave her alone to make her own decisions, to make her own mistakes. Even this total stranger was trying to butt into her private life.

Slowly, she began to regain control of her emotions. Rolling over onto her back, she looked up at the ceiling. She began to realize that she was not being fair to him. What was wrong with her, she asked herself? Why was she blaming Tony for anything? He had done nothing but show his concern for her. He had not only taken her in, but he had most likely saved her life. If he had not helped her, she would have died in the parking lot all alone.

Her thoughts of what Tony had done for her made her realize that she owed him at least an explanation. That much he deserved for all he had done for her. But giving it some thought, she also realized she owed him more then that. She owed him her life.

She sat up on the edge of the bed and looked toward the door. Marcie felt the need to go back downstairs and apologize to him. She not only wanted to apologize to him for not answering his questions and for running away, but for ruining his perfectly good dinner.

Marcie stood up and looked in the mirror. Her eyes were a little red and puffy from crying. There was nothing she could do about that now. It struck her as a little funny that she was worried about how she looked. She looked better now than when he found her, cold, wet and covered with snow. She turned away from the mirror and opened the bedroom door.

Just as she stepped out of the bedroom into the hallway, she heard the front doorbell ring. She stopped dead in her tracks. Her first thought was that her manager or the police had discovered where she was hiding and had come for her. She wanted to move back into the bedroom to hide, but her legs would not let her move. Marcie wondered if Tony would tell them that she was here. She could hear Tony as he answered the door.

"Oh, hello," she heard him say.

The tone in his voice told her two things. First, it was someone he knew, and second, it was someone he was not really all that anxious to see, at least not right now.

"May I come in?"

The voice was a little familiar to her. Marcie had heard that voice somewhere before, but could not place it. Suddenly, it came to her. It was Linda Forrest's voice that she was hearing.

"Yes."

The tone in Tony's voice showed no emotion at all. It was just a flat, unemotional reply to her question.

Tony stepped back and held the door as Linda stepped into the living room. He shut the door behind her, then just stood there waiting for her to say what was on her mind. It was apparent to Linda that Tony was still upset with her. She waited for him to offer to take her coat, but he did not offer.

"I think we should talk," Linda said.

"Okay. What do you want to talk about?"

Tony knew perfectly well why she had come, and what she wanted to talk about. He really did not want to talk to her right now, but decided that this was as good a time as any. It was a talk that they were going to have to have sooner or later. It was just as well that they get it over with now.

Linda looked over his shoulder and glanced around the room. She was looking for some sign that the woman she had seen him with at the mall was here. She walked over to the sofa and sat down.

"I think we need to talk about this afternoon," she said looking up at him.

"What about this afternoon?"

Tony knew what she was getting at, but he was going to make her bring up the subject. He did not think he owed her any explanation after the way she had acted. After all, Linda was the one who stormed off down the mall. She was the one who had been rude to Mary.

"I must admit that I was rather surprised to see you with that woman hanging on your arm. She just sort of hung on you. She wasn't even all that pretty. Her hair was plain, and she didn't have any makeup on. I wouldn't think of going out in public without some makeup. I would have thought you'd have had better taste. Where in the world did you find her, anyway?"

Tony listened to her as she rattled on, but all he could think of was how much she sounded and acted like his ex-wife. His ex-wife had that same kind of superior, arrogant attitude; and had judged people on how they looked, rather than on what they were like. He never liked that about his ex-wife and he didn't like it any better coming from Linda.

Tony was beginning to think that it had been a good decision for him to put off asking her to marry him. He was so absorbed in thinking about how much she was like his ex-wife that he did not really hear her question.

"I asked you a question."

The tone of her voice reminded him of the way the television lawyers sounded when they are demanding a response from a hostile person on the witness stand. He wondered if attorneys took a course in how to question witnesses.

"Tony!" She raised her voice a little to get his attention.

"Oh. I'm sorry."

"You were not listening to me. I asked you a question."

"I'm sorry," he said casually. "What was the question?"

"What is the matter with you?"

It was easy to see that she was becoming annoyed with him. Linda liked being in control of any situation and she seemed to be losing her control of him.

"Nothing. Nothing's the matter with me."

"You seem so distant. You're not listening to me at all."

"Maybe that's it," he replied thoughtfully. "Maybe, I'm tired of listening to you tell me how it's going to be. Maybe, it's time that you listened to me for a change."

"What?"

Linda was shocked to hear him talk to her that way. He had never talked to her like this before. Tony had always been what she thought was the perfect gentleman. He had never demanded that she be quiet and listen to him, but had always let her say what she wanted to say.

"Tony, what has gotten into you?"

"I've been thinking a lot about us lately," he said ignoring her questions. "I don't really think we are right for each other."

The look on her face was that of total shock. Her chin dropped and her eyes got big as she stared at him. She could not believe what he was saying.

"But, we have been talking for months about getting married," she finally was able to say. "I don't believe you really mean what you are saying."

"That's just it, I do mean it."

"It's that woman."

"It's not "that woman"," he replied. "And WE have not been talking about marriage at all. YOU have been talking about marriage for months. YOU have been telling me where we will live, how we will decorate the house, even the kind of house we will live in. YOU have not once asked me what I want, or what I think."

"It's all that, that woman's fault!" she said sharply.

The anger in her voice could be felt all the way up the stairs. Marcie had not wanted to listen in, but she could not help herself. She wished she had never come here with him. She had made a mess of her life, and now she was making a mess of his.

"It's not "that woman's" fault." It's my fault for not saying something a long time ago. We are just not meant for each other. It's better to find out now, than for us to make the same mistake I made with my first marriage. By the time I realized the mistake, it was too late and we are both unhappy."

"She has poisoned you against me!" she yelled at him.

"Now that's not true and you know it. I think it would be best if you were to leave. We can talk more, if you want, when you have had a chance to think about it and have had a chance to cool down a little," Tony said without raising his voice.

Tony was trying to keep a calm voice. It was clear there would be no way to reason with her as long as she was so upset and irrational.

"You had better think about what you said. If you think I'm going to put up with this kind of playing around, you better think again," she said as she stood up.

Tony wanted to tell her that he was not playing around, but in her current state of mind his words would have landed on deaf ears. He simply stepped back and opened the door for her. She stormed out the door and down the sidewalk to her car. Tony shut the door, but continued to watch her as she got into her car. The car slid on the snow packed street as she tried to speed away.

Tony wished her no harm and hoped that she would not have an accident on her way home, but he was glad to see her go. He was sorry she was so upset, but it was better that they break it off now then to drag it out.

Tony turned away from the door and looked toward the stairs. He wondered if Mary had heard them fighting. If she had, he hoped it had not upset her, too.

Tony thought about going upstairs and having a talk with Mary. He even thought about apologizing to her for asking her too many questions, but decided against it. With the luck he was having trying to explain things so far this evening, maybe it would be best to just let things lay for a while.

Tony decided that he would go to the kitchen and finish cleaning up. It would give him a chance to think and keep his hands busy at the same time.

CHAPTER SIX

Marcie heard the front door close as Linda left. Her first thought was to go downstairs and tell Tony that she was sorry she had caused a falling-out between him and his girlfriend, but she decided against it. She thought that it might be better to just go back to her room, at least for now. Maybe, Tony would like to be alone for a while, she thought.

Marcie turned around and stepped back into her room, quietly closing the door behind her. She leaned back against the door and closed her eyes. Her mind was full of confusion.

"What's wrong with me?" she asked herself out loud.

She was feeling like everything she touched, or had anything to do with, was turning sour. In her eyes, her life was all a big mess; and now she was making a mess of Tony's life, too.

Marcie knew deep down in her heart that she had to do something about her life. After all, that was the reason she had run away in the first place. Maybe, if she got her own life on track; she would get out of Tony's life, and he could get his life back together again.

She pushed herself away from the door and went over to the bed. Dropping down on the bed, she wrapped her arms around one of the large pillows. Holding the pillow tightly against her breasts, she rolled over on her back and looked up at the ceiling. She tried to concentrate on resolving her own problems. There were a ton of questions she needed to answer for herself. What was she going to do about this tour? She knew in her own mind that she could not continue unless she wanted to have a nervous breakdown. How was she going to explain to her manager that she could no longer continue to tour the country doing one night shows without a break? How was she going to explain it to her fans? How was she going to get out of her contract in the hope of getting back to living a more normal life?

Each time she tried to think about one of the questions she needed to answer, her concentration was interrupted with thoughts of Tony. It was becoming very frustrating for her. She could not think of her own problems without also thinking of Tony.

Marcie tried to rationalize her confusion and her inability to concentrate. She was sure the reason she could not think here was because this was Tony's house. Everything in the house made her think of him. She was surrounded by him. Maybe, it would help if she took a long walk in the park across the street, she thought. She did not feel like she was truly alone here. She was too easily distracted.

Marcie pushed the pillow off to the side and sat up. After taking a deep breath and letting it out slowly, she stood up and walked to the door. She opened the door and listened, but she did not hear anything. She walked down the stairs to the living room, but did not see Tony.

Just as she sat down and picked up one of her boots, Tony came out of the dining room.

He stopped and watched her as she slipped her foot into the boot.

"Are you going somewhere?"

Marcie jumped at the sound of his voice. She had not seen him come into the living room. She turned and looked up at him.

"Yes. I thought I would go for a walk in the park."

"Okay if I come with you?"

"I really would like to be alone for a little while, if you don't mind."

The tone of her voice was almost apologetic. She knew she needed to be alone, but to refuse him the opportunity to go with her after all he had done for her seemed somehow wrong. She briefly considered changing her mind.

"I understand. I often go for a walk in the park when I need to be alone to think," he said with a smile. "Enjoy your walk."

She tried to look into his eyes to see if he really meant what he said. Did he really understand or was he just trying to be nice? She could not tell, but something deep within her told her that he did understand.

As she slipped her other boot on, she watched him walk over to the front closet. He got out the warm coat that he had bought for her. As she stood up, he held the coat for her. Slipping her arms into the sleeves of the coat, she pulled it around herself and zipped it up. She was feeling a little sorry that she had told him that she wanted to be alone, but she also knew she would not be able to concentrate on resolving any of her problems if he was with her. She turned and looked up at him.

"Enjoy your walk," he said in an effort to assure her that he knew it was important for her to be alone right now.

All of a sudden she wanted very much for him to go with her. She was about to ask him to come along with her when he reached out and opened the door for her.

"I'll have some hot cocoa for you when you get back. You will probably need it. It's cold out tonight."

Once again, he was showing his concern for her. He must understand, she thought. She decided that at least this once she would go alone. Maybe, some other night they could go for a walk in the park together.

"I really do need this time alone," she said softly. "I have some things I need to sort out."

The thought occurred to her that her feelings for him might be one of the things she needed to sort out. She tried to push that thought aside. After all, she didn't know him very well.

"I understand, really. I sometimes go for walks when I need time to think. Take your time, but don't get too cold, and be careful," he said.

Marcie stepped up close to him. She rose up on her tiptoes and gave him a quick, light kiss on the lips.

"Thank you," she said softly.

Tony looked down at her. He had not expected her to kiss him. He watched her as she turned and went out the door. It seemed strange to him that such a light, tender kiss would touch his feelings so deeply. He waited until she was off the porch and starting down the sidewalk before he closed the door.

Marcie walked down the steps to the sidewalk. She sensed that he was still watching her. Her lips had hardly touched his, yet she could still feel the warmth of his lips. She had intended for it to be just a simple "thank you" kiss, nothing more; but it seemed to go much deeper than that, at least for her. She had come out to think and hopefully resolve some of her problems, but that one little kiss seemed to make things more complicated than ever for her.

She crossed the street and entered the park without looking back. The light from the streetlights sparkled on the fresh snow like a million tiny diamonds sparkling under a bright light. Although the sun had set hours ago, the lights reflecting off the snow seemed to give the park a soft glow. The branches of the large pine trees drooped with the weight of the snow on them. There were small animal tracks in the snow where animals, like squirrels and rabbits, had run from one tree to another looking for food.

A walking trail wondered through the park. She walked along it until she came to a large pond, almost like a small lake. She noticed several ducks and a few geese on the pond. It had not gotten cold enough to freeze the pond solid and force the birds off the pond. The birds must have decided to stay the winter, she concluded. She was sure that the visitors to the park were keeping the birds well fed.

Slowly, she walked around the pond as she tried to concentrate on her problems. The harder she tried to keep her thoughts on the tour and her problems as a singer, the more she thought about Tony. Gradually, she came to the conclusion that she would not be able to separate the two. The two had become one in the same problem. She would not be able to deal with one without dealing with the other.

The one thing she had decided was that she would not be able to continue this tour. She just could not continue to go from town to town, never having a life of her own. She could not continue to let other people run her life. The more she thought about it, the more she was convinced of what she really wanted, of what would really make her happy.

She wanted a life away from the glitter and noise of the stage. Marcie wanted a life that included a husband and possibly children. She wanted a family that she would not have to leave to go out on tour. She wanted a family where they had evening meals together, went to school plays, helped the children with their homework and spent time together. She could not do that if she was on the road all the time. She wanted to settle down and make a life for herself.

Her thoughts quickly turned to Tony. She wondered if he was the type of man that she was looking for. He certainly was nice, kind and very generous. She wondered if he liked children. She knew from his conversation with Linda that he had been married once before, but she did not know if he had any children as a result of that marriage.

"My God, girl, what are you thinking of? You don't even know this man," she blurted out loud to herself.

Marcie stopped in her tracks and looked around. She was afraid someone might have seen her talking to herself and think she was crazy. It was not only that, she was afraid someone might have actually heard what she had said. She didn't know why it mattered, but for some reason it did.

After she was sure no one was around, she continued her walk. Her mind filled with thoughts of Tony and questions she would like answered. Many of the questions she would ask him were very basic. What does he do for a living? What are some of his likes and dislikes?

It suddenly popped into her mind that he might not have any interest in her at all, other than that she was another human being who needed help. Maybe, he was just trying to help her. He seemed to be a very honest and straightforward sort of man.

Marcie instantly realized she had not been entirely honest with him. She had not really lied to him, but she had not told him the whole truth about herself, either. Would he be as accepting of her if he knew her stage name was Marcie Roberts and she was a country western singer? Would he understand why she had not told him? Could he deal with the publicity that she had caused by running away in the middle of her tour?

She began to wonder if it wouldn't be best if she just returned to the tour. That thought caused her to shiver. She could not return to the tour and allow everyone else to run her life again. Marcie had this deep feeling that if she returned to the show, she would be trapped there. There might never be another chance for her to take control of her life again. This was her chance to take back her life, and that was just what she was going to do.

She walked along a little further until she came to a bench under a streetlight. Marcie brushed the snow off the bench and sat down. She leaned forward resting her elbows on her knees and her chin in her hands. Looking down at the ground directly in front of her, she watched the light sparkle on the snow as she tried to sort out her feelings, her desires and her thoughts. She tried to make some sense out of all the things that were running through her head.

Tears began to fill her eyes as she thought about Tony. He was so good to her and was giving her what she needed most right now, time and space. He could have easily found a reason not to let her go alone, but he gave her the space she needed. She wondered why she had not met someone like him years ago. If she had, she would not be here now, trying to put her life back together.

Marcie was so wrapped up in her thoughts that she did not see the old man walking along the edge of the pond, but he saw her. He stopped and watched her for a short time from a distance.

It seemed to him that she was very unhappy, or that maybe something was wrong. He walked up to her.

"Excuse me, Miss, but are you all right?" the old man asked.

She had not heard him come up beside her. His voice startled her and she jumped at the sound of it.

"I'm sorry, Miss. I didn't mean to frighten you. I saw you sitting here alone and thought, maybe, something was wrong. Are you okay?"

This old man seemed very concerned. His eyes sparkled in the light. For some strange reason, this old man reminded her of her grandfather. Maybe, it was the gray overcoat he wore. It was just like the one her grandfather liked to wear in the winter. Maybe, it was the way he looked at her, or maybe the concerned look in his eyes. Maybe, it was the gentle tone in his voice. Whatever it was, she was not afraid of him.

"I'm okay. Thank you," she said with a forced smile.

"Are you sure?"

"Yes. I'm fine, but thank you anyway."

The old man started to walk away, but stopped. He slowly turned around and looked back at Marcie. She was already deep in thought again. He studied her for several minutes. The old man was sure he knew who this woman was. He had to find out. He walked back toward her. As he approached, she raised her head and looked up at him.

"Excuse me again, but I have to ask this. Are you Marcie Roberts, the country singer?"

Marcie hesitated as she looked into his deep brown eyes. She thought about telling him the same thing she had told Tony, but something deep down inside her told her not to lie to this man.

"Yes," she replied softly.

"I thought so. Do you know there are a lot of people looking for you?"

"Yes. I know."

"A lot of your fans are worried about you. I would venture to guess your parents are worried about you, too."

"I'm sure they are."

"I guess that you have a lot on your mind right now. I'm sure you don't need some meddling old fool standing here running off at the mouth. I'll be on my way. I'm sorry to have disturbed you."

Marcie did not respond, but simply watched the old man as he turned and began walking away. She thought about what he had said. There would be a lot of people worried about her. It just did not seem right to have people worry about her because she needed time to think.

"Sir, wait, please," she called out to him.

The old man stopped and turned around. A broad smile came over his face as Marcie stood up and walked toward him.

"I don't want people to worry about me. But, I need time to think."

"Shall we walk while we talk? My circulation is not very good any more, and I get cold if I don't keep moving."

"Sure."

Slowly, they began to walk along the edge of the pond. She told the old man about her life as a singer. She had a need to tell someone, someone who at least seemed to care, and this old man seemed to care about her. She knew that sometimes it is easier to talk to a complete stranger, someone that you may never see again, than to talk to someone close.

He listened to her as she talked. It was easy for him to understand her need to have someone who would just listen. He was alone most of the time and had no one to talk to, or to listen to him. The old man knew that if she got it all talked out, she most likely would solve her own problems with little or no help from him or anyone else.

"I understand what you're saying," the old man said smiling at her.

"You do?"

"Yes. Many years ago, I made a decision to put all my time and effort into my career. I made a good deal of money. I've had a pretty good life, but the one thing that I missed out on was the joy of having a family."

"I don't want to miss that."

"You don't have to. You can do whatever you set your mind to do. Don't let other people run your life for you. It's fine to listen to them and to hear what they have to say. But then you should do what is best for you," he advised.

They walked a little further before she stopped. She looked at the old man's face and smiled.

"I have to go now. Thank you for taking the time to listen to me."

"I enjoyed our little walk," he replied with a smile.

"I need some time alone now. I have a good deal to think about. Thank you again."

The old man smiled and nodded that he understood. Marcie turned and began walking away. Her mind was full of the advice that the old man had given her. She had heard this same advice before, but hearing it again gave her a new slant on her own problems. She was able to look at things in a little different light, and to ask herself some very pointed questions. Did she really want a career in singing, or did she want a family? Was it possible for her to have both? Did she really want both?

As she walked across the park toward Tony's house, she wondered if the old man would report that he had seen her. If he did, what would he tell them? She was confident that he would not tell them where he saw her, but simply report that she was fine and would be contacting them when she was ready. She wasn't sure why she felt this way, but the old man had seemed to be very understanding, he seemed to know what she needed to hear.

Her thoughts once again turned to Tony. He had been very nice to her, to say the least. She searched her feelings about him. The more she thought about him, the more she wanted to be with him. She knew she liked him very much, but was this feeling she could not control her love for him? Did she love him, or was she just grateful that he had saved her life? She would have to let time answer those questions, she decided.

Marcie also decided that she would have to tell Tony who she really was if there was any possibility of building any kind of a lasting relationship with him. If he liked her enough, he would understand why she didn't tell him in the beginning. She could not help but wonder if she was making the right decisions.

As soon as Tony's house came into view, she stopped and looked at it. She was suddenly feeling like a schoolgirl who was crazy about a boy who didn't even know she existed. Only this was different, he did know she existed and she was not a schoolgirl. She could not help herself. She wanted to be near him. She wondered what it would be like to be held by him. It was not hard for her to remember how that light kiss had affected her.

She wished she knew how he felt about her. If he just liked her a little, it would at least be a place to start.

CHAPTER SEVEN

Marcie walked across the street toward the house. The house seemed to loom up in front of her almost daring her to enter. She was almost afraid to go up the steps to the porch. Once on the porch, she closed her fist and reached out to knock on the door. She hesitated. Closing her eyes, she tipped her head back as if to say a short pray.

Marcie could not help herself. For just a brief second or two, she felt as if she was doing the wrong thing. Staring at the door, she wondered what was behind it for her. Would she find happiness, or would she find nothing but disappointment? Was it possible that the answers she was seeking were behind the door, or was this going to be just another one of her mistakes?

The time had come for her to take charge of her life and to make her own decisions. It was time to take the risk, to step forward and go after the life she wanted for herself. It was time to knock on the door.

Marcie raised her hand again, knocked on the door and waited. It seemed like it was taking forever for Tony to answer the door, but within a few seconds the door opened and Tony was standing there looking at her. A soft pleasant smile came over his face when he saw her.

She let out a silent sigh of relief. The look on his face told her that he was glad that she had returned. It was not much of a sign, but at least it was enough to let her know that he wanted her to be here with him, and that gave her hope. She was suddenly flooded with deep feelings for him, feelings she would need to control at least until she knew how he felt about her.

"Come in," he said as he stepped back and held the door for her.

Marcie returned his smile, then walked past him as she stepped inside. She heard the door close behind her, but she could not turn around and face him until she was sure that she had her emotions under control. If she looked into his eyes right now she might not be able to control herself and she might throw her arms around him and hang onto him.

"May I take your coat?" Tony asked softly.

Marcie felt his hands on her shoulders as he reached up to help her take off her coat. She took in a deep breath as she let him slide her coat off her shoulders and down her arms.

"Would you like that cup of hot cocoa?"

She took in a deep breath before turning around to face him, but he had turned around to hang up her coat and had his back to her. She looked at him. Tony was being very polite and very nice to her, but in her mind he was showing no real interest in her. A wave of disappointment suddenly washed over her.

Tony turned back toward her and looked into her eyes. He could not understand what he was seeing, but it concerned him deeply. She seemed as confused now as when she had left for her walk.

"Are you all right?" The tone of his voice showed his concern for her well being.

"Yes," she replied softly.

He did not accept her answer at face value. Tony felt that she might not be telling him the whole truth. Something was troubling her. But then, she had gone for the walk to help her sort out things so she could make some kind of a decision.

It seemed apparent to him that she had not been able to resolve her problems and make the necessary decision. He wanted very much to know what it was that was troubling her, but felt she would tell him if and when she was ready.

"Okay, then how about that cup of cocoa?"

"Great. It's very cold out there," she answered with a soft smile.

Marcie turned toward the kitchen as Tony approached her. As he started past her, he took her hand in his. He didn't even look at her, he simply took hold of her hand. His hand felt warm to the touch, but it also sent a warm feeling through her entire body. She felt as if she was getting mixed signals from him. One minute he seemed distant, the next, warm and tender. She looked up at him out of the corner of her eye as they walked to the dining room.

They passed through the dining room and on into the kitchen. He led her to the small breakfast table where he pulled out a chair for her. She let go of his hand and sat down on the chair. Tony poured two cups of hot cocoa and carried them to the table. He set a cup in front of her and one across from her, then sat down across the table from her.

Tony watched her as she wrapped her hands around the warm cup and lifted it to her lips. She carefully took a sip of the hot liquid. After taking a sip, she looked over the rim of the cup at him and smiled.

"It's very good," she said softly.

"Thank you. I'm glad you like it."

They sipped their cocoa in silence. Tony watched her, hoping that she had reached some sort of decision on what was troubling her. She seemed to be thinking very hard about something as she stared at her cup for what seemed to be a very long time. It concerned him.

"Is there something I can help you with?"

"What?"

Marcie suddenly looked at him as his question had startled her. She had not really heard his question, but she knew he had asked her something.

"Is there something I can do to help you?"

She looked into his eyes and wondered if he was truly concerned about her, or if he was just being nice to her. She needed someone to talk to, someone that would at least listen to her without being judgmental and without being critical of her.

"I guess I need someone who will just listen to me."

"I make a very good listening post," he said with a smile.

She smiled back at him. Something about him told her that he would listen to her and not try to tell her what to do. She was still a little afraid to tell him who she really was for fear that he would not want to get involved in her problems. She hesitated, but if she was going to have any hope of a somewhat normal life, she was going to have to start now.

"I'm not who you think I am," she started out nervously.

"You're not Mary Robertson from Ohio?" he said with a bit of surprise.

"Well, yes I am. Well, sort of."

"Okay, but I'm afraid you're going to have to explain that one to me. You are Mary Robertson, but you're not."

"This is kind of difficult. I was Mary Robertson, but I'm now Marcie Roberts. I changed my name a few years ago."

Marcie watched his face for some sort of reaction, but saw no change in his expression. She wondered if he had known all along, or if he just didn't know who Marcie Roberts was.

"Why didn't you tell me you are Marcie Roberts?" he asked calmly.

She looked up from her cup and looked into his eyes. His eyes did not tell her anything about what was going on in his head. She had wanted to talk to him, to get to know him a little before she told him everything.

"I guess, I wanted to be just plain Mary Robertson for a little while. I had to get away from the tour long enough to figure out what it is I want out of life."

Marcie paused for a second. She had been trying to figure out how she was going to tell him who she was without making him angry with her for lying to him, but it was too late to worry about that now.

"I thought if you knew who I was, I wouldn't get the chance to be alone to work things out."

"Have you worked things out?" he asked flatly.

"No, not really," she had to admit.

"How much longer do you think you will need?"

Tony tried not to make any big deal out of who she was. He simply wanted her to do what she had to do. He was almost trying too hard not to influence her to do one thing over another.

Marcie was sure that he was angry with her for lying to him. She had hoped to avoid this, but it wasn't to be. She just knew that there was little hope in building any kind of a relationship with Tony now. It was over and there was nothing she could do to win his trust in her. There was no sense wasting any more of his time, or hers, for that matter. She let out a deep sigh.

"I won't need any more time. If you don't mind, I'll just stay tonight and leave in the morning," she said, disappointed with how things seemed to be turning out.

The tone of her voice was that of someone who had just given up. She did not wait for a response. She simply set her cup down on the table, pushed her chair back away from the table and stood up. She looked over at Tony as if she were waiting for him to ask her not to leave. When he said nothing, she simply turned and left the room.

Marcie went directly to her room. She shut the door behind her and flopped down on the bed. Nothing seemed to be going her way. No matter how hard she seemed to try, everything went wrong. She was not happy on the tour and it was not going well. She finally met a man that she could possibly love, if she didn't already, and she ruined any chance of building a lasting relationship with him. All she could think about was how much of a mess she had made of her whole life.

She was feeling very depressed and could not keep herself from crying. She buried her face in her pillow so Tony would not hear her crying.

Tony cleared the table. Marcie continued to fill his mind. He could not stop thinking about her. Yes, she had lied to him, but had she? She had told him that she was Mary Robertson from Ohio, which she was, or at least had been. But, she was also Marcie Roberts, the singer. She should have told him that, too, but was that so important, he thought. He had the chance to meet and know the real person, not the stage image. He had found the real person was interesting enough.

After cleaning up the kitchen, Tony went into the living room and dropped down on the sofa. His mind continued to place a picture of her in his head. He began to try to think of all the positive things about her that he could, making mental notes. She had beautiful soft hair, her eyes were warm and loving, her complexion was smooth and soft, and she had a very nice figure. She even looked good in a sweatshirt and jeans and no makeup.

Those were her physical traits that he liked. What about her, he asked himself. She seemed to be a very sensitive and emotional person. He was sure that she was a caring and a very giving person, especially of herself. Her self-image seemed to be a little weak right now, but he felt that would not be unusual given the circumstances, whatever they were. He also believed that she would like to be a very private person, but her position as a very popular country western singer made that almost impossible.

Tony thought about this for quit some time. He was sure that it was this conflict between wanting to be a very private person and being a person who was always in the limelight that was causing her this inner turmoil. He thought about going upstairs to see if she would talk to him about what it was that was troubling her. Tony was sure he knew, but if he was going to try to help her, she would have to want his help.

He started toward the stairs, but when he got to the stairs he decided that he would not bother her, not just yet. Instead, he would give her some time to herself. He returned to the living room and sat down on the sofa and turned on the television to watch the evening news.

The news had already started. On the television screen was a picture of Marcie Roberts. The anchorwoman was giving the latest news on the disappearance of Miss Roberts.

"The official word is that Miss Roberts has been resting in seclusion with a mild case of the flu which has affected her voice. It is reported that this tour has been officially canceled. However, her promoter has stated that once Miss Roberts is released by her doctor to sing again, she will start her next tour. Her promoter also said that her next tour would begin here in Denver. He said he added Denver to the beginning of her next tour so that her fans will not miss out on seeing her.

"However, we have learned from another source, very close to Miss Roberts, that she simply walked away from the tour while the stage was being set up in McNichol's Arena.

Miss Roberts has not been heard from since, and her whereabouts is unknown.

"Our source tells us, Miss Roberts did not want to have this tour scheduled in the first place. It seems that Miss Roberts had just completed a six month long tour on the east coast and needed to rest her voice. She was not happy with her promoter for scheduling this western tour so close to the other. Apparently, she was unable to convince the promoters to end the tour because she was tired and she needed to rest."

Tony listened with a great deal of interest. She must have been very, very unhappy to risk her life to get away from the tour, Tony thought. Just being unhappy didn't seem to be enough of a reason for a normal person to risk their life. It had to be more than that, he concluded.

Tony tipped his head back and closed his eyes. What would make someone risk everything, including their life? The most obvious things, like fame and fortune, came to mind first. He immediately rejected those as her reasons because she had them already.

The fact that she was unhappy with the way the tour was going might be a contributing factor, but certainly it was not reason enough.

Someone controlling her life, telling her how and when to do things could be a strong possibility. He thought about this one for a while. This one could very well be the reason, he thought. It certainly would be for him. He needed to have at least some control over his own life, and he was sure she would feel the same way.

It was difficult for him to try and put himself in her shoes. He was not familiar with the music business, but he didn't think she was the type of person who would let someone run her life for her for very long without rebelling. He was sure that was what she was doing, rebelling in the only way she could.

The more he thought about her, the more he began to understand why she had not told him the complete truth. She had made it clear that she needed time to think, to make decisions about herself and her future. If he allowed her to leave before she had her problems worked out, he would be the one placing restrictions on her. He did not wish to become part of her problem, but preferred to be part of her solution. He felt he should give her the time she needed, even help her if he could.

He sat up and looked toward the stairs. This would be as good a time as any to tell her that he would help her in any way he could. He stood up and went up the stairs to her room. Knocking lightly on the door, he waited for an answer.

Marcie rolled over and looked at the door. She was not sure that she wanted to talk to anyone just yet. However, she thought it might be considered rude to not answer the door for her host.

She rolled off the bed and went over to the door. Slowly, she opened the door to find Tony standing in the hall.

"I'm sorry. I just wanted you to know that you can stay as long as you want. I also want you to know that if you need someone to talk to, I will listen and not tell you what to do. I'm here for you."

Although it was not what Marcie expected, she sensed that Tony had meant every word he said. She also noticed that his voice seemed soft and gentle, something she was not used to hearing in a man's voice.

"Thank you, but I still think I should go in the morning. I have caused enough trouble for you."

"No, you haven't. I mean, you haven't caused me any trouble at all. In fact, you saved me from making a very big mistake."

"I don't understand."

"If it hadn't been for you, I might have married Linda. You gave me the chance to re-examine that relationship. After I did, I discovered I didn't like where it was going. I owe you for that. Will you let me help you, please? Oh, there is one other reason that you do not have to go."

"What is that?"

"It just came over the news, your tour has been officially canceled. You see, you don't have to leave at all."

She looked at him in disbelief. Was he really telling her the truth? He seemed to be truly sincere. She needed some time to think about it.

"Could I have a few minutes to think?" she asked softly.

"Sure," he said with a smile. "I'll be downstairs."

"Okay," she replied as she slowly shut the door.

Marcie could hear his footsteps as he went down the stairs. She turned around and looked at her reflection in the mirror on the dresser. It was clear that she had been crying, again. She sat back down on the edge of the bed to think.

Her mind filled with thoughts about the tour and what would happen once she got back to Nashville. As far as this tour was concerned, it was over. However, once she got back to Nashville she would be reprimanded by the record company. Most likely she would get threatened with a lawsuit for failing to complete the contract that her agent had her sign without completely disclosing all of the terms. And her promoter would also threaten her with a lawsuit for failure to complete the tour.

Marcie was sure that the lawsuits might never come about if she returned to Nashville and immediately got back on a tour, but she just couldn't do it any more. Her agent and her promoter had taken advantage of her, along with her attorney. Her attorney was the biggest crook of the three because he was there to protect her interests in contract negotiations, but he had advised her to sign a contract that was not in her best interest. It was a contract that gave all the rights to the promoter and her agent. She knew now that she never should have trusted any of them, but with all the legal details in a contract of this type, she needed a lawyer.

The woman in the mirror needed someone's help, too. It had become obvious that she would not be able to clear things up without help from someone she could trust. It was also clear that she wanted Tony to understand what she was going through. With all the problems that she had finding someone to trust, why was it she felt she could trust Tony?

She thought about Tony for a few minutes, and about this whole evening. He had given her space and time to think without putting any pressure on her. More importantly, he had forgiven her for not telling him the whole truth. He had also told her that she didn't have to leave at all.

So many of her decisions would depend on how Tony felt about her, and how she felt about him. If there was nothing between them, maybe it would be better if she just returned to Nashville. Once she completed the two remaining years of her contract, she would not sign a new contract and simply disappear from public view. She could take all the time she needed to decide her future then. She was not sure that she could handle two more years of one tour right after another, but that might be her answer.

On the other hand, if he did have feelings for her, it would be a little more complicated. They would have to make decisions together. She wondered if he would stand by her for two more years. They would have to plan their future, but that would be okay as long as they did it together.

Marcie had to make a decision. Was she going to find out how Tony felt about her, or was she going to tell him that she was returning to Nashville in the morning? She had run away because everyone else made decisions for her. Twice in the same day she was going to have to make a decision for herself. Now was the test to see if she could make some of the really tough decisions that she was going to have to make.

The decision to let Tony help her was no small matter. She would be facing the possibility of rejection by him, the one thing she was sure would be the hardest thing in the world for her to accept. At this point, she had no idea how he felt about her. The only clue that he might have some feelings for her came from the fact that he seemed to care what happened to her.

Marcie took in a deep breath, put her hands together in front of her face and said a silent prayer that the decision she was making was the right one for her. She let out the breath and stood up. Turning toward the door, she reached for the doorknob at the same time she reached her decision. She was going to find out how Tony felt about her if it took all night. With her new resolve, she started downstairs.

Tony turned as he heard her coming down the stairs. He watched her as she entered the living room. Once in the living room, she stopped and looked at him. The look on her face was that of a scared child, a child that had just done something terrible and was about to be scolded for it.

"Come, sit down with me." Tony said softly.

She looked at him, then slowly walked across the room toward the sofa. Marcie sat down next to him, but could not look at him so she stared at the blank television screen. Her mind was running a mile a minute as she tried to think of what to say, and how to ask him to help her.

Tony was worried about her. He wanted to let her know that she could talk to him about anything, but he did not want to push her. He had already told her that he would listen, now it was time to do just that.

Marcie had her hands folded together in her lap. Tony reached out and put his hand over her hands. She turned and looked into his eyes. His eyes seemed to plead with her to tell him her troubles. They seemed to give her the courage she needed to share herself with him.

"I need someone to talk to," she said in a whisper.

"You can talk to me."

The soft sincerity of his voice helped reassure her. The look on his face also assured her that he would listen and he would do what he could to help her.

Marcie started off slowly by explaining to him how she got into the music business in the first place. She began from the time she got her first contract until now. How her first contract had been a routine contract, a rather normal contract for someone just starting out in the business. She told him about her last contract and the changes that had been made in it by her agent and her attorney. How she felt that she had been manipulated by a crooked agent and a greedy promoter with the help of an equally greedy attorney.

"Were the changes in your contract made before or after you signed the contract?" Tony asked.

"I can't say for sure. I don't remember the contract I signed including so many tours. It is not like me to add that many tours to my schedule, especially tours that would keep me away from home at Christmas time."

Tony thought about it for a minute. Now that she was very popular and was drawing large crowds, they might have worked out a contract with hidden clauses that would make her go from one tour to the next. Tony figured, at first, her agent and her attorney had looked out for her interest, but they got greedy when she started to make it big. She had trusted them to do right by her, but in the last contract they had looked out only for themselves. Oh, she made a lot of money, but they made sure they got a lot more than their share.

Tony had listened to her every word. He was getting angry as he thought about how they had taken advantage of her to line their own pockets. Tony was sure that her contract would not be binding if they could prove it had been tampered with or actually changed after she signed it.

Tony had several friends who were attorneys. He was sure that any one of them would be willing to look into this for him. However, Tony needed to know what Marcie really wanted?

"I have some friends who might be able to help you. What I need to know is what do you want? Do you want completely out of the contract, or do you want to change the contract to reduce the number of tours you have to make? What is it you want?"

She looked up at him. Marcie did not know what she wanted. At least she was not sure what she wanted. She had too many questions running through her mind to give him a this or that type of answer. Right now, sitting beside him like this, she wanted to stay right here with him and never leave his side. But she wondered if he wanted her at his side.

Tony saw the confusion in her face. He sensed that she might not have had time to figure out just what she wanted. He was sure she needed more time to make that kind of a decision.

"It's getting late. You have some very tough decisions to make. Why don't we relax and watch an old movie on television tonight. We can take another look at the problem tomorrow after you have had a chance to rest. How's that sound?"

"That sounds good to me," she answered with a sigh of relief.

Marcie was beginning to feel a little better already. She was at least going to have someone to help her with her trouble. With his help, she had a feeling that everything might work out all right after all.

Marcie watched Tony as he got up and left the room. She heard him go upstairs and wondered what he was doing. Within a few minutes, he returned with a couple of big pillows and a large quilt.

"I thought we might spread out here in front of the sofa and get comfortable."

She kind of liked the idea and stood up to help him spread out the quilt. He handed her a pillow and set his up against the sofa to lean back against. She set her pillow up against the sofa next to his while he picked out a movie on one of the late night movie channels.

After they got comfortable and had been watching the movie for a while, Tony put his arm around behind her. With his hand on her shoulder, he gently pulled her up against him. She rested her head on his shoulder.

It did not take long before she had fallen asleep. He did not wish to disturb her, he liked her against him, but he needed to get some rest, too. When he caused her to move so he could get more comfortable, she slid down and laid on the floor. He slid down beside her, reached across her and pulled the covers over her. As he covered her, she rolled up against him. He wrapped an arm around her as he settled down on his pillow.

CHAPTER EIGHT

It was still dark when Marcie first opened her eyes. She remembered being on the floor with Tony, but she was a little disoriented for the moment. It took her a second or two before she realized that Tony was curled up against her back. She could feel Tony's arms wrapped around her and the warmth of his breath in her hair. She could not tell if he was awake or not, but from the rate of his breathing she was pretty sure that he was still sleeping.

For the first time in a long time, Marcie was feeling very secure and safe. The floor was not the most comfortable place she had ever slept, but it was not all that bad, either. She was also beginning to feel good about herself for the first time in a very long time. Here she was lying on the floor with a man she hardly knew, but who must care a great deal about her. Why else would he have covered her with the comforter to make sure she stayed warm? Why else would he wrap her in his arms and hold her close to him to keep her safe and secure?

She smiled to herself. This is the way I would like it to be, she thought. It had been a long time since anyone had held her so close. She had missed being held.

Marcie lightly ran her hand over the back of Tony's arms and held them close to her. She was happier at this moment than she had been for a very long time. Wrapped in the warmth of Tony's arms, she slowly closed her eyes and drifted back to a peaceful and relaxing sleep.

* * * *

Once again Marcie opened her eyes, only this time she found herself curled up against Tony's side. Her head was resting on his shoulder and her arm lying across his chest. His arm was behind her head with his hand resting lightly on her shoulder. She could hear his heart beat in a smooth, strong rhythm. His chest rose and fell with each breath. She wanted to look up at him, but did not want to wake him if he was still asleep.

It was not until Marcie felt Tony stir a little that she raised her head off his shoulder and looked up at him. He smiled at her.

"Morning," he said softly.

"Morning," she replied sheepishly.

Marcie was feeling a little embarrassed, but she did not understand why. She had slept all night with him on the floor, but they had done nothing for her to be embarrassed about. She sat up, straightened her sweatshirt and ran her hands through her hair in an effort to make herself look a little more presentable.

"I must be a sight," she said.

"I think you look beautiful in the morning."

She looked over at him. He could see by the look on her face that his compliment had embarrassed her.

"How about some breakfast?" he asked in an effort to change the subject.

"I would like that. I'll pick up the living room while you fix breakfast."

"Sounds like a good trade off to me," he replied as he sat up.

Tony stood up and reached down to her. He took her by the hands and helped her to her feet. She stood in front of him looking up and waiting, but for what she did not know. For a minute, she wondered if he was going to kiss her. He was looking deep into her beautiful blue eyes.

"May I kiss you?" he asked softly.

It was almost as if someone else had asked the question. It didn't even sound like Tony's voice.

"Yes," she replied in a whisper.

Tony let go of her hands and reached out to her. He put his hands on her narrow waist as she reached up and put her hands on his shoulders. As he gently pulled her closer to him, he tipped his head down to meet her. She tipped her head back to meet him. Their lips met in a soft, warm kiss. As he kissed her, he wrapped his arms around her and pulled her tightly against him. She slid her hands up over his shoulders, behind his head and held him to her as they kissed.

Suddenly, their kiss was rudely interrupted by the loud noise of someone knocking at the door. It startled both of them. They instantly let go of each other as if they were school kids caught doing something they were not allowed to do.

Marcie quickly straightened her sweatshirt and tried to catch her breath. Tony hesitated for a few seconds before he started for the door. Just as he reached for the doorknob, he hesitated again and looked back to where Marcie was, but she had gone. She was retreating to the other room. He waited for her to step around the corner. As soon as she was out of sight, he opened the door.

Standing on the front porch were two rather big men and a somewhat smaller man. The little man was wearing a rather expensive suit under a very expensive topcoat.

"Are you Mr. Anthony Beckman?" the little man asked.

"Yes. What do you want?"

"We received a tip that Marcie Roberts is here in this house. I want to talk to her."

He had the confidence in his voice of someone who always got what he wanted.

"Who are you?"

"I am Frank Alexander. I'm Miss Roberts' promoter."

Tony took an instant dislike for this man. He also did not like the idea that this little man was attempting to intimidate him by bringing along two big thugs.

"Well, Mr. Alexander, I don't believe that Miss Roberts wishes to talk to you right now. If you'll leave your card, I'll be more than happy to see that she gets it. She can call you when she is ready to talk to you."

"I don't think you understand," Mr. Alexander said in a rather threatening tone.

"No, I don't think you understand, Mister," Tony quickly interrupted him. "I don't know how it is where you come from, but as long as Miss Roberts is here in my house, she will be able to do as she wishes. Right now, she doesn't wish to talk to you.

"She will talk to me," he insisted.

"I don't know who you think you are, but you're on my property, Mister. I think it would be in your best interest if you were to leave before you find yourself in a lot more trouble then you can handle. Should Miss Roberts wish to talk to you she will, but not until she's ready. You understand that?"

"You can't keep me from talking to her."

"I can as long as she doesn't wish to talk to you. This conversation is over. You better take your two goons and get off my property before you find out what the inside of the Denver Jail looks like."

The little man stood there for a second looking at Tony. It was clear that Tony was not intimidated by him or his thugs. There was nothing Mr. Alexander could do right now, outside of breaking the law. Since he didn't know who Mr. Beckman was or who he was associated with here in Denver, Mr. Alexander decided it would be best to simply leave for now. He turned to leave, but stopped and turned back toward Tony.

"Mr. Beckman, I would suggest that you explain to Miss Roberts that she is in a lot of trouble. If she doesn't return to Nashville very soon, she will find herself with a very big lawsuit, plus she will be out of a career."

"I'll be sure to tell her."

Tony stood in the door while he watched the three men go down the sidewalk and get into a rather large luxury car. Only after they left did he shut the door and turn around.

Marcie was standing in the doorway to the dining room looking at him. He could tell by the look on her face that the men on the porch had frightened her. Tony walked up to her and took her in his arms. He hoped that he could comfort her at least a little.

Marcie laid her head on his shoulder. What she had expected to happen was indeed going to happen if she did not return to Nashville soon. She knew that what Mr. Alexander had said about a lawsuit, he meant.

Tony could feel the tension in her as he held her. He did not know what he could say that would help make her feel safe again. All he could do for her now was to hold her.

Suddenly, a thought ran through his mind. He took his arms from around her, put his hands on her shoulders and looked her in the eyes.

"I've got an idea. Why don't we have breakfast? We can figure out just what we will do after we have full stomachs. I think better on a full stomach. What about you?"

She looked up at him as if he had suddenly gone crazy. She was about to be sued if she didn't leave and return to Nashville right away. Her life was a real mess and it looked like it would get worse before it would ever get better, and all he wanted to do was eat. However, she did like the fact that he used the word "we". At least she had the feeling that she was no longer alone. For the first time in as far back as she could remember, she had someone who was willing to help her. She had no idea what he could do, but it was nice to know that he was willing to try.

Tony was smiling down at her, waiting for her answer. She could not keep from smiling back at him.

"Okay," she conceded.

"Good. You pick up the living room while I fix us a good breakfast."

Tony kissed her lightly on the forehead, then went into the kitchen. She paused for a second. Maybe, he was right. There was no sense trying to figure all this out on an empty stomach.

Marcie went on into the living room. After picking up the pillows and stacking them on the sofa, she picked up the quilt and folded it up. She stacked the pillows on the quilt, then gathered them up. She took the pile of bedding up the stairs. Since it had not come from the room she had been using, she assumed that it had come from his room. She pushed open the door to his room and went inside.

Marcie stopped cold in her tracks. She had never seen a room quite like this one. It was like stepping back into the past one hundred years or more. The entire room was done in old antiques.

The bed looked like a large old four-poster feather bed. The quilt on the bed was typical of those handmade quilts made like her grandmother had done. At the foot of the bed was a large wooden chest.

She set the pile of bedding on the chest as she looked around the room. On the hardwood floor were several handmade rag rugs, one on each side of the bed and one in front of the large mirrored dresser. Along one wall was an old armoire, or freestanding wardrobe closet.

The room reminded her of something she might find in a museum, yet it seemed to be very functional, very warm and very comfortable. She was sure that it had been Tony's idea to do the room this way. Marcie could not picture Linda Forrest wanting a bedroom like this. She was more the white walls and chrome type. Why would he do just one room in this fashion, she asked herself? But then why not? If it was what he liked, what was wrong with it? After all, this is his house.

The more she looked around, the more she liked it. Everything, from the rag rugs on the floor to the old style lamps on the dresser fit the decor. It looked inviting. It certainly had character. She smiled as she turned and left the room. Just as she closed the door, she heard him call her to breakfast.

"Breakfast is on."

"Coming."

She hurried down the stairs to the kitchen. Marcie could smell the bacon and eggs. She scooted onto a chair at the table just as he was setting her breakfast down in front of her.

Tony smiled as he sat down across the table from her. He noticed that she seemed happier, or at least a lot less depressed then she had been.

"Dig in."

"I put the pillows and quilt on the chest at the foot of your bed," she said as she watched him for some sort of reaction.

"Thank you. You didn't need to take them up. I would have done that."

He did not change his expression one tiny bit. She was sure he knew that his bedroom was rather unusual, especially since the rest of the house was very much a modern house. She decided she would take a different approach.

"What's it like to sleep on a feather bed?"

"I see you noticed that my bedroom is a little different from those found in most houses," he said as he smiled at her from across the table.

"I noticed, but what's it like?"

"Very comfortable, if the feather bed is a good one."

"Is it a good one?"

"Most certainly. I'll bet you're wondering why I have one room in this house decorated like that one? It's simple," he said without waiting for a response. "The furniture in that bedroom belonged to my great grandmother. Her husband, my great grandfather, built every piece of furniture in that room for her as a wedding present. When I had this house built, I had one room set aside for that furniture."

"Did your ex-wife like it?"

"No. She hated it. I had all the furniture stored while I was married to her. I bought this house after my divorce."

Marcie realized she had gotten into an area of his life that he might prefer not to talk about, although he didn't seem to be holding anything back. She should probably change the subject, but she wanted him to know how she felt about the room.

"I like your room. It seems so warm and comfortable."

Tony was not sure if she was just being nice, or if she really meant what she said. He continued to eat his breakfast and hoped she had meant what she said. They finished their breakfast without much conversation. They each became engrossed in their own thoughts.

It did not take long before Tony's thoughts turned to Marcie and her trouble with her promoter. He wondered if she had given any more thought to her problems. He was hoping that whatever happened, she would stay, at least for a while.

Marcie's thoughts had turned to her problems, too. She knew she would be sued as soon as she got back to Nashville, even though her promoter had indicated he would not if she returned right away. However, that was not the problem she wanted to deal with right now. She didn't want to go back to Nashville. She wanted to stay here in Denver and sleep in the big feather bed with Tony.

She surprised herself a little thinking about sleeping in the feather bed with Tony. It was not like her to want to go to bed with a man that she hardly knew. In fact, it was not like her to want to go to bed with a man she did know without some kind of long-term commitment, like marriage.

Tony could see that she was deep in thought. He did not want to disturb her, but he felt the sooner they faced her problems, the better.

"I hope you don't mind, but I called a friend of mine while you were upstairs. He's an attorney for a big corporation here in Denver. He said he would come over this afternoon, if you would like to talk to him."

"I guess it would be okay. I don't know what he can do."

"I don't either, but one thing I do know is that we can trust him. He will tell you the truth and help you if he can. He'll also tell you if he can't."

Tony reached across the table and took her hand. Her hand was small and soft. He looked into her eyes as she looked back at him.

"You can stay here as long as you want," he assured her.

A warm smile came over her face. That simple comment from him was all she needed to help her make the decision to stay.

"I would like to talk to your attorney friend," she said as she looked into his eyes.

Tony smiled as he lifted her hand up and kissed the back of it. He let go of her hand, stood up, went directly to the phone and placed another call to his friend.

Marcie began clearing the table while Tony was on the phone. She watched him as he wrote notes on a pad next to the phone. When he hung up the phone, she stopped what she was doing and turned toward him.

"He will be here for lunch. Jeff wants you to sit down and write down as much as you can remember about your contract. He wants things like the percentages your agent, promoter, and attorney get, the number of tours you are required to take, that sort of thing," Tony explained.

"What's that for?"

"I guess he is looking for something that's not consistent with other contracts in your business. I'm not really sure. All I know is that's what he wants."

"Well, I can try."

"He also wants to know what was explained to you about your contract by your attorney before you signed it."

Marcie nodded that she understood what was being asked of her. She was not sure what good it would do, but she would try to write down everything she could remember. The one thing she was sure of was that she was going to be sued, anyway.

Tony took her by the hand and led her into the dining room. He motioned for her to sit down at the table. She sat down and waited for him as he went to his desk and began looking for paper and pen. Within a few minutes, he returned with the paper and a pen and set it down in front of her.

"I'll leave you alone for a while. You may be able to think better without me sitting here."

Marcie smiled up at him. She did not know what good this was going to do; but if Tony thought it was worth a try, she would do the best she could. He leaned down and kissed her lightly on the forehead, then turned and left the room.

Marcie looked down at the paper and pen lying on the table in front of her. She tried to think about her contract, but her thoughts kept returning to Tony. He was really trying to help her get out of this mess. She liked him a great deal and she was becoming more and more convinced that she even loved him. But, did she feel this way about him because he had saved her life, or because he was trying to help her get out of her contract? She wondered why she loved him.

Marcie began to wonder what her motives were for staying here. Was she really trying to get out of this contract? Did she really want to get out of the music business? Did she love this man, or was she using him as an excuse to escape?

The sudden thought that she might be using Tony sent a wave of guilt through her. It had not occurred to her that she might be using him without realizing it. It filled her mind with more questions.

She knew that in the beginning, when she first met Tony in the parking lot, she was not using him and she had not planned to use him.

In fact, the thought that she may have been using him had not entered her mind until now. She silently reviewed what had happened over the past couple of days. Tony had been kind to her, gentle and considerate of her and her feelings. He had been everything a woman could want in a man. She decided that she had not been using him, and from this day on she would make a conscious effort to make sure that she didn't start.

He had finished cleaning up the kitchen and went into the dining room to see if he could be of any help to her. She looked up at him. He could not tell what she was thinking, but the look on her face worried him. It looked as if she might cry at any moment.

"What's the matter?"

The tone of his voice showed how much he was concerned about her. It also made it very clear to her that he cared very much for her. She could not stop the single tear that slowly rolled down her cheek.

"Nothing, nothing at all," she said as a smile came over her face.

Tony reached down and gently wiped the tear away. He did not know why she was crying, but her smile seemed to make it all right.

"Sit with me," she said.

Tony pulled up a chair. He noticed that she had not written a single word on the paper. Looking up at her, he wondered if she was having difficulty facing the task at hand.

"Will you help me? I don't know what he really wants."

"Sure," he replied.

For the next hour or so, Tony asked her questions about her contract. He knew a little about contracts. After all he dealt with them all the time. Tony knew little about her type of contract, but at least he had enough knowledge to ask questions on how it compared to contracts that other singers had with their agents. Tony made notes for her as she talked about what her agent, her promoter, and her attorney had told her. They also discussed the differences between the actual contract and what she had been told. He wrote down all the differences she could think of on the paper.

Once they had finished, Tony pushed back his chair and looked at the paper. He was no lawyer, but it was easy to see that the contract was a very good deal for the people who were supposed to be working to protect her interests. It was also clear that the only interests they were protecting were their own.

"I don't know what Jeff can do for you, but I know him. He'll make it very difficult for them to collect even if they do sue you."

"I hope a lawsuit can be avoided."

"I hope so too. The only ones who ever win are the lawyers."

Marcie nodded in agreement. She reached out and put her hand over his.

"Have you decided what you want?"

"I have some ideas of what I want. The one thing I want now is to get out of this contract. I would like to spend some time away from the tours and away from the public. I would like to have the freedom to meet people and, maybe make some friends. I miss having a normal life," she tried to explain.

Marcie was afraid to go any further in trying to tell him everything that she wanted. She wanted to stay here and get to know him better, but that was not entirely true. Deep down in her heart, she was already sure that she loved him. It was her head that she was having trouble convincing. What she really wanted was time to find out if he shared her feelings. She needed to know if there was a chance for them to have a lasting relationship, together.

"I guess we are ready to talk to Jeff," he said as he dropped the pen on the table.

"I guess we are," she agreed. "I think I will go get cleaned up and fix my hair before he gets here."

Tony nodded as she pushed back her chair and stood up. Watching her as she left the room and went upstairs, he wondered if he might be able to get her to stay with him for a while at least. He let out a sigh and knew he would just have to wait and see what happened.

Tony went upstairs to his room. He decided it might be a good idea if he cleaned up a little, too.

CHAPTER NINE

Tony returned to the living room after taking time to shower and shave. He changed into slacks that were comfortable and looked good on him. The shirt he wore was a long sleeved shirt with the sleeves rolled up a couple of turns. It was dressy enough to look nice, yet casual enough to be comfortable. He sat down in the living room and waited for Marcie.

It was not long before Marcie returned to the living room, too. He glanced toward her as she entered the room. She was wearing the blue slacks and the flowered blouse he had gotten for her.

It was impossible for him not to look her over. The slacks fix her very well, showing off the smooth curved lines from her narrow waist and on down over her hips and legs. The flowered blouse accented her upper body as well. The complete outfit showed every curve of her very nice figure. She had fixed her hair so that it cascaded down onto her shoulders, framing her beautiful face in yellow gold.

A smile of approval came over Tony's face. Marcie responded by returning his smile. She was pleased that he found her pleasant to look at and that he apparently like what he saw. It sent a warm, wanted feeling through her. It was a feeling she had missed for some time. She had seen men look at her before, but this was different. He was not lusting after her, but rather desiring her. In her mind, there was a very big difference.

Marcie also took a minute to look him over. After all, fair is fair, she thought. She saw a very handsome man in front of her. His dress slacks fit him well, showing off his narrow waist. His dress shirt fit him well, too, accenting his broad shoulders. His dark brown hair and deep brown eyes seemed to draw her to him.

She briefly wondered if she would think he was so handsome if he had not been so kind and gentle to her. That thought quickly dissolved from her mind as she began to walk toward him.

Tony stood up, reached out and took hold of her hands.

"You look beautiful," he whispered as he looked into her clear blue eyes.

"Thank you," she responded with an even bigger smile.

He turned and motioned toward the sofa. After she had sat down, he sat down beside her.

"What time is your friend coming over?"

"He said he would be over about noon."

"What are you planning to have for lunch?"

"I've got some tuna. We can have tuna sandwiches, if that's okay?"

"That would be fine with me."

Tony was about to say something else when he heard a knock at the door. Tony glanced at his watch as he stood up.

"He's a little early."

Tony went to the door. As he opened the door, he was surprised to find Linda Forrest standing on his front porch. She looked at him with a very serious look on her face. The look in her eyes was that of pure hate.

"I would like to talk to you," she said.

The tone of her voice was sharp and raw like the cold steel of a knife. That, along with the look on her face, made it clear that this was not going to be a pleasant visit. Just by the way she was standing with her feet firmly planted, and the way she made her statement reminded Tony of the television programs where the attorney is about to question a very hostile witness on the witness stand.

"I don't really think that we have anything more to discuss. I think it was all said yesterday," Tony said calmly and clearly.

Tony had no regrets in breaking off their relationship. He had hoped that breaking off with her would be clean and without any problems, but it was beginning to look like she was not going to just simply let it go. He did not want to get nasty with her. After all, they had had some very good times together.

"Yesterday, I didn't know who that woman hanging on your arm was, but I know now," she stated flatly.

"I don't see what difference that makes."

"You will in a minute."

"No, I don't think so. I don't think there is anything you can say that will make any difference."

"Oh really?" she replied with a venomous tone in her voice and a smug look on her face.

"Well for your information, the firm I work for has been hired to represent Mr. Alexander, her promoter. I asked to handle this case."

Tony was surprised to hear this bit of information. He knew that Mr. Alexander would be hiring a lawyer, but did not think it would be so quickly. He also did not expect him to use a local law firm since he was from Nashville and had lawyers there. But what really came as a shock to him was the fact that Linda would take this case since she had a personal interest in one of the parties.

Another thing that surprised Tony, but not as much, was the pleasure that Linda seemed to be getting out of this whole situation. If he hadn't been sure about breaking up with her before, he certainly was now. She had just confirmed for him that he had made the right decision when he decided that Linda was not the one for him. She was not only bossy, like his ex-wife, she was a spiteful, vindictive and a darn right mean person, as well. It was obvious that she was going to use this opportunity to get even with him for dumping her.

Marcie had heard part of the conversation. She got up and walked up behind Tony. As she stood there, she took hold of Tony's arm.

"I see you still have her hanging on you," Linda said as she glared at Marcie.

Tony could see the hate Linda had for Marcie. He was not about to put up with her snide remarks and her arrogant attitude.

"I have heard quite enough from you."

"You haven't heard anything, yet," she interrupted. "Mr. Alexander is filing suit against little Miss Roberts to the tune of five million dollars. How's that grab you?"

Tony could feel Marcie's grip on his arm tighten. He had to agree that five million dollars was nothing to sneeze at. But he was not about to let her know what he thought of it, nor was he about to be intimidated by threats, especially from Linda.

Tony had about enough of this and was not going to stand for any more. He was getting very angry, but he did not know if he was angry because Linda was using this to get back at him, or because she was trying to intimidate him. Either way, he did not like it.

"Unless you have some kind of legal papers to serve Miss Roberts, I strongly suggest that you get off my property and stay off it before I pick you up and throw you out into the street."

Tony spoke slowly and clearly so that not one word would be misunderstood. He wanted her to know that he meant every word he said.

Linda had never seen Tony so mad. He had always been sort of quiet and even tempered. The tone of his voice and the fire in his eyes told her that she was just inches away from being literally tossed out in the street.

"Papers will be served. I can assure you of that," she countered sharply as she stepped back away from him.

"Well, until they are, I do not want to see your face on my property. Do you understand?" he asked as he took a step toward her.

Linda did not say anything more. She had pushed him about as far as she dared. She simply looked from Tony to Marcie as she backed up.

Linda could not see what Tony saw in this woman. She was nothing but a common showgirl to Linda's way of thinking. Linda looked back at Tony, then turned and walked off the porch.

Tony stood in the doorway with Marcie as they watched her leave. As soon as Linda got into her car, he turned and looked down at Marcie. He could tell by the look on Marcie's face that she was very worried.

"I wouldn't get too excited about her. She's just using this as a chance to get back at me for yesterday," he said in an effort to make Marcie feel better.

Marcie wanted to believe him, but it was hard. She knew the type of man Mr. Alexander was, and he would not let her go so easily. After all, she was his major source of income, his meal ticket.

She was also beginning to understand what type of woman Linda was, a vengeful and angry woman. Marcie tried to smile for Tony, but it was not a very convincing smile.

Tony put his arm around Marcie as he closed the door. He led her back to the sofa. He wanted to say something that would make everything better, but he had no idea what to say. He wanted to protect her from all this unpleasantness, but he could not do that, either.

Yet, even though he wanted to protect her, he knew deep down that she could probably handle anything that came her way. All she needed was a good reason, something to fight for and something that would give her some hope. He was convinced that she was not as frail as she appeared.

"Jeff should be here before long. He might have an idea or two that will be of some help," Tony said as he tried to reassure her that everything was going to be all right.

Marcie wanted to believe him, but she was having a great deal of difficulty. She hoped Tony's friend, Jeff, would be able to help, but she didn't think he would be able to provide any hope of a settlement she could be comfortable with.

Marcie was tired of everything. She was tired of being on the road all the time, tired of the hassles with her promoter, her agent and her own attorney. She was tired of not being able to live the kind of a life she wanted. But most of all, she was tired of fighting for every little bit she did get. She let out a deep sigh as she sat back down on the sofa. She just wanted to have it over and done with. To be able to sit down, relax and put it all behind her.

Tony wanted her to relax, too. He wanted her to clear her mind of all her problems, at least for a little while. He could see the worried looked on her face and wanted so much to be able to make this whole thing easier for her, but he knew he could not do that. All he could do right now was to sit down beside her and be there for her.

He sat down with her, reached around behind her head and put his hand on her shoulder. He gently pulled her up against him, letting her rest her head on his shoulder. He could feel her body gradually relax and the tension drain from her.

She could hear the steady rhythm of his heartbeat as she leaned against him. It seemed to help her relax. She rested her hand on his leg as she closed her eyes. She was not tired or sleepy, but she was weary. She felt as if she might be able to draw strength from him, the strength that she would need to get through all this, and still keep her sanity.

Marcie felt comfortable leaning against Tony. She could still remember how safe and secure she had felt in his arms last night. All her worries and problems seemed to just disappear.

A firm rap on the door suddenly startled her. Sitting up quickly, she looked at Tony. He could see that the rap on the door had frightened her. He was sure she was wondering if Linda had returned.

"It's okay," he assured her. "It's probably Jeff this time."

Leaning forward so that Tony could get his arm out from behind her, she watched him as he stood up and walked over to the door. She glanced at her watch and realized that she must have dozed off for a few minutes. She heard Tony greet someone at the door. She stood up as Tony and another man entered the living room.

"Marcie Roberts, I would like you to meet my good friend Jeff Duncan. Jeff, this is Marcie Roberts, also known as Mary Robertson."

"I'm pleased to meet you," Marcie said with a bit of a smile.

"I am pleased to meet you, too. I only wish it could have been under more pleasant circumstances. I hope you don't mind my saying so, but I am one of your biggest fans."

"Thank you."

"What do you say we sit down at the table and have a little lunch? We can talk over lunch," Tony suggested.

"That sounds good to me. I would like to get to know Miss Roberts a little before we get into contracts and all that legal stuff," Jeff said to Tony

Marcie simply nodded in agreement. The three of them went into the dining room. Marcie and Jeff sat down at the table and began talking while Tony went into the kitchen to prepare some sandwiches.

After Tony had set their lunches on the table, he joined them. He listened as they talked about Marcie from the time she first got into the music business until now. He could see that Jeff was listening very carefully to her every word. He had heard bits and pieces of her life before, but he was interested in hearing more about her.

After they had finished eating, Tony cleared the table while Jeff and Marcie continued to talk about her current contract. They were comparing her current contract with her former contracts and with what Marcie had learned about other singers' contracts when Tony returned to the table. He sat down next to Marcie and put his arm over the back of her chair.

She glanced over at him and gave him a brief smile. It was clear that she was pleased to have him at her side. She liked the interest that he took in her and his willingness to stand by her when she needed his support.

Jeff had listened very carefully to everything that Marcie had told him. He could understand her desire to get out of her latest contract. It was apparent to him that if what she told him was correct, then her attorney had not looked out for her interests at all.

"I don't want to build your hopes up too high, but I think you have a pretty good chance of getting out of this contract."

Marcie looked over at Tony and took hold of his hand. She squeezed it as she smiled at him. It was easy for her to see that Jeff's comment had pleased Tony, too.

"Marcie, can you get me your copies of both your former contract and your current contract?"

"Yes."

"Good. I need to take a good close look at both of them and compare them with the contract your attorney should have. If what I believe is correct, I will go after your attorney."

Marcie looked a little puzzled. "Why are you going after my attorney? I thought you would go after my promoter."

"It looks like we would have a better chance of going after your attorney for malpractice. If we can prove that he was not keeping your interest first, we can put the burden on him. We may still have to go after your promoter, and possibly your agent. If they are all in this together, and we can prove it, we can get you out of this contract."

"What if my attorney will not give you his copy of my contract?"

"First of all, I have to know if you want me to represent you?" Jeff asked.

Marcie looked over at Tony then back at Jeff. "Yes. Yes I do."

"As your new attorney, he does not have a choice. If he doesn't turn it over to me, I will file a suit against him."

"Does that mean that they will not be able to sue me?"

"No, not really. They may sue you anyway. If we can prove that your attorney was not protecting your interests, but was protecting his own, I don't think they will be very willing to try to sue you. They will most likely be looking for a way to cover their own asses, ah, excuse me, behinds," Jeff said.

"Are you aware that her promoter has hired a law firm here in Denver to represent her promoter, and that Linda has taken on the case?" Tony asked.

"Linda? Your Linda?" Jeff asked in surprise.

"Linda Forrest," Tony said correcting him.

Jeff noticed that Tony had not referred to Linda as 'his Linda'. Jeff looked from Tony to Marcie. He could see that there was something special between these two. It was something he had not seen between Linda and Tony in the years that he had known them. He wondered if his friend, Tony, had fallen for Marcie, and if she had fallen for Tony. The way they looked at each other indicated to Jeff that there was much more between them than simply friendship.

"I find it very hard to believe that she would even consider taking on a case where there is such an obvious conflict of interest," Jeff said shaking his head.

Jeff knew Linda to be a very good lawyer. He had always considered her to be above reproach and felt that she was honest, knowledgeable, and would not do anything that could be considered even close to unethical. He wondered what could have prompted her to take this case.

"Well, she did. I think she did it to get back at me."

Tony went on to explain about the chance meeting they had with Linda in the mall. Tony also told him about Linda coming over and going into a rage when Tony told her that their relationship was over. He told Jeff about her coming over a second time, just a little while ago, to tell him that she was representing Marcie's promoter and about how she seemed to enjoy the chance to get back at him for dumping her.

Jeff had not been one of Linda's friends. In fact, he did not like her very much. It was mostly because of the way she treated Tony, his best friend. He had never said anything to

Tony, but he was glad his friend had dropped her. Jeff had a feeling Linda was the type of person who could be very vindictive if she put her mind to it. However, he did not realize she would use her position as an attorney to take revenge against someone who had made her angry.

"I must admit that I am disappointed in her. I never really liked her, but I did think she was a very good lawyer who would not purposely misuse her trust as an attorney so cheaply," Jeff replied.

"I didn't think she would either."

"I'm sure we can get her off the case," Jeff said.

"No. I think it is about time for her to find out that she can't have everything the way she wants it. She has been very successful in resolving the cases she has been given by her firm. I think it is time she finds out what it is like to have a real fight on her hands," Tony said.

"I have to admit that she has had a charmed life as an attorney," Jeff said thoughtfully.

"Well, how does our case look, and will you take it on?" Tony asked.

"If the contracts are like what I've been told, and if you are willing to go to court, I think there is a very good chance we can get you out of this contract. Are you willing to go to court?" Jeff asked as he looked over at Marcie.

Marcie looked from Jeff to Tony. It had been hard for her to deal with all the pressures of one-night stands all over the country. It had almost driven her to a nervous breakdown. She had almost killed herself in a parking lot in her attempt to get away from it all. She had no one to turn to then, no one to help and support her at that time.

Jeff and Tony sat quietly waiting for Marcie's response. They knew it was going to be a difficult decision for her. She had been under a great deal of pressure, and they knew it was not going to be an easy fight to free her of this contract.

It was different now, Marcie thought. She had an attorney who was willing to help her, a man who would give her the support she needed, and a reason to fight her way out of a bad contract. For the first time in many, many months, she felt as if relief from all the pressure was in sight. She had something to fight for.

"I'm ready," she said as she drew in a deep breath.

"Good. I'll get started on an injunction to keep Linda's law firm from bothering you, at least until I have had a chance to read and study your contracts. Then, we will go from there."

"That sounds good to me," Tony replied.

"Me, too," Marcie added.

"Where can I get hold of you if I need to talk to you?"

Marcie looked at Tony, then back at Jeff. She wanted to say he could get hold of her here, but she was not sure she should say that as Tony had not offered to let her stay with him indefinitely,

"You can get hold of her right here. She will be staying with me at least until this is over," Tony injected.

"Good. I'll be in touch," Jeff said as he stood up.

Jeff picked his coat up off the sofa and put it on. Tony and Marcie stood up and followed Jeff to the door.

"I would like to thank you for the opportunity to meet you. I only wish it could have been more pleasant for you," Jeff said to Marcie.

"I'm glad to have met you, too."

"I'll see you later," Jeff said to Tony.

"Thanks for coming on such short notice."

"Hey, what are friends for," Jeff said with a smile. "Besides, wait until you get my bill."

"It will be worth every cent," Tony assured him.

Tony held the door as Jeff left. As soon as Jeff was off the porch, Tony shut the door and turned toward Marcie. She looked tired. He was sure that this had put a heavy drain on her. He walked up to her and put his arm around her shoulder.

"Are you all right?"

"Yes. I think I would like to rest for a little while. I guess I'm still not fully recovered from the other night."

"Why don't you go take a nap while I get some work done in my study. Maybe after dinner, we can take a walk in the park, if it's not too cold. We could even take in a movie," he suggested.

"I would like that. It has been a very long time since I've been to a movie."

"Good. We'll take in a movie after dinner."

Tony walked her to the stairs. He took her in his arms and kissed her lightly on the lips. The kiss was warm and gentle. He then took his arms from around her and watched her as she turned and went up the stairs. As soon as she was out of sight, he went into his study to work on one of his design projects.

CHAPTER TEN

Tony sat down at his drafting table in the study. He reached up and turned on the large overhead light above the table. Spread out in front of him were the partially completed plans for the remodeling of one of the lower downtown buildings near the site of the new baseball stadium. He leaned forward on the table and looked over the drawing. He was satisfied with what he had done so far, but realized that he had not worked on it for past few days. He had not worked on it since the night he found Marcie in the parking lot at Mile High Stadium.

He picked up one of his many drafting pencils as he studied the design. Without making a single mark on the drawing, he laid the pencil back down on the table. Pushing his chair back away from the table, he turned to look out the window. His head was so filled with thoughts of Marcie that he did not notice it had started to snow again.

Tony was pleased that his friend, Jeff, had come over and talked with Marcie. Jeff had done a great deal to build up Marcie's spirits and self-confidence. Now she had hope for the future. There were no definite answers yet, but things were at least beginning to look up.

If Marcie could get out of her contract, she would have a number of options open to her. She could return to Ohio and start to build the kind of life she wanted. She could go back to Nashville and find herself a good attorney and promoter who would not try to work her to death. The one important thing was that she would be free to do whatever she wanted to do, even stay here in Denver if that was what she wanted to do.

Tony liked the idea of her staying in Denver. It would give him a chance to be near her. There was no doubt in Tony's mind that Marcie was a beautiful woman, and there was also no doubt that she had some problems. But it was the way she handled herself that fascinated and drew him to her. He was sure there was a very special person down deep inside her. If some of the pressures of her life could be removed, maybe that special person would come to the surface. She had shown him, in her own way, that she could be a very independent person. In some ways, she was very independent, yet in other ways, she was very dependent.

It struck Tony as a little funny, but she sort of reminded him of a cat he had many years ago. It was a strong willed and a very independent cat as long as it had the security of a good home and a loving family to look out for it. But, when it was left alone for long periods, it would become nervous and scared. He smiled as he thought of that old cat and how much it had been like a human.

Tony was sure he was falling in love with Marcie, but he did not know how to let her know. He thought about simply telling her that he loved her, but was afraid that it would just put more pressure on her. She didn't need that right now. Whatever she decided to do with her life would have to be her decision, without any pressure from him.

He realized that there was little he could do if she decided to return to Ohio or Nashville. No matter how much he wanted her to stay here in Denver, he could not allow himself to do anything that would pressure her into staying. It had to be her choice.

He would just have to spend some time with her doing those things that other people do, the things she had missed out on over the years. If they had enough time together, she might decide for herself to stay here. He wanted her here with him, to hold, to love and protect. But he also knew that if she was to return his love, he would have to give her the space she needed, and the time she needed. If he didn't, she might feel that he was smothering her. He would never want her to feel that way.

Tony considered his thoughts carefully. He would spend time with her, but he would also give her time to be by herself. Besides, he would need time to himself. It would be necessary for him to search out his own feelings for her. He would also need time to work on his designs.

That thought quickly reminded Tony that he had a design on his drafting table that was in need of his attention. He would have to get to work on it, or he would not have it ready in time for the meeting with his client to consider it.

His client was a very important man. If this design for the remodeling of one of his client's buildings was accepted, there would be a strong possibility that Tony would be hired to do the design work for his other buildings.

Tony turned around and pulled his chair up to the drafting table. He once again picked up the drafting pencil. Only this time he began working on the design. Within a few minutes, Tony was once again engrossed in his work. Building design had always been a dream of Tony's and now he was making his living at it.

* * * *

It was dark when Marcie opened her eyes. She was lying across her bed with her arms wrapped around her pillow. As she held the pillow against her breasts, she thought of Tony. She found it easy for her to bring a picture of him to her mind. He was not only handsome, but he was kind and gentle. He seemed to care about her and seemed to want her to be with him.

For the first time in a very long time, she had some small degree of hope that her future would not be made up of one or two night concerts in a long list of nondescript cities across the country. It looked as if she might be able to get out of her contract. She was well aware of the consequences of her decision to try to void her contract. If successful, it would make it far more difficult for her to get offered a contract by another firm.

That thought did not seem to bother her very much. She had always enjoyed singing, even before she was being paid to sing. If she sang just for her own enjoyment, and maybe for Tony's, that would be enough to keep her happy. She wondered if Tony had ever heard her sing. She wasn't even sure if he liked the type of music she normally sang.

She rolled over on her back, still holding the pillow to her breasts. Everything she seemed to think of lately included thoughts of

Tony. The more she thought about her future outside of the music business, the more she thought of him. She was beginning to realize there might not be much of a future for her at all without Tony being a part of it.

Marcie was beginning to realize just how much she loved him. She loved him more than anything else she could think of, even more than her music, and music had always been a very important part of her life. The thought of loving someone that much scared her. She could not remember ever loving anyone that much, except for maybe her mother, but that was different.

She sat up and looked toward the window. The drapes were closed. She laid the pillow on the bed, stood up, went to the window and pulled the drapes back. She looked out at the snow as it floated down to the ground. The snow seemed to sparkle in the light of the street lamp. The tracks that had been in the snow were now covered up leaving a fresh new covering of pure white.

Though she did not really believe in such things, she wondered if the fresh covering of snow might be some sort of omen. If it was, it must be a good omen, she thought. The fresh snow seemed to help light up the park, taking it out of complete darkness. Her thoughts returned to when she was a child in Ohio. She had always liked to go walking when it was snowing like this.

She wondered if Tony liked to walk in the snow. Thinking of Tony made her wonder where he was and what he was doing.

After a brief stop in the bathroom, she left the room and went downstairs. She did not see Tony in the living room or in the dining room. Then she remembered that he was going to his study to do some work. She suddenly realized that she had no idea what he did for a living.

She went to his study where she found the door open. Marcie could see that he was working on something on a large drafting table. She stood in the doorway and watched Tony for several minutes, not making a sound. She did not want to disturb his concentration. While she waited, she glanced around the room. On the walls were pictures of old buildings, several of them. She was sure he had something to do with them, but he was far too young to have had anything to do with their construction.

There was one picture of an old building that caught her eye. As she studied the picture, she realized that the building had been modernized, renovated. Yet, it had retained its original look very well.

"Hi," Tony said softly.

She quickly turned and looked at him. She had been so engrossed in the picture that she had not seen him turn around.

"I'm sorry. I did not mean to startle you."

"That's okay," she replied with a sheepish smile.

"Did you sleep well?"

"Yes, very well. Is this building around here?" she asked.

Tony glance toward the picture she was looking at.

"Yes. That is an old building in lower downtown. It had been used for a warehouse for the past thirty or forty years. Just two years ago it was bought and renovated. The man who bought it is now using it to house his workshop where he makes solid oak furniture. His furniture is all custom made or made to order, and it is very expensive.

"He had the upper floor renovated into his living quarters. It's a very nice place," Tony explained.

"Is that what all these pictures are, pictures of buildings that you have renovated?" she asked as she moved about the room looking at some of the other pictures.

"I don't renovate them. I simply work up designs for the contractors based on how the owner wants to use the building. Some want to put shops in them, some want to convert them to living spaces, some want to simply restore the building. I work up designs that keep the style and the original design of the building intact while making the building more functional for its intended purpose."

"That sounds fascinating. Did you do designs for all these buildings?"

"Yes."

Tony was proud of the work he had done to preserve some of the older buildings in the area and to make them useful again. It pleased him even more that Marcie seemed to be interested in what he was doing. He continued to watch her as she admired his work. As she approached his drafting table, he turned in his chair and pushed back a little so she could see what he was doing.

"What is this design of?" she asked as she stood beside him and looked at the drawings on his drafting table.

"This is the layout of the second story of an old building just off Colorado Boulevard. The first floor is to be used for several different shops while the second and third floors will be living quarters."

For the next few minutes, he showed her how the rooms were going to be laid out. She listened to him as he explained what he did and what the contractors had to do to complete the project.

"That's very interesting. I didn't know it took so much planning to renovate one of these old buildings."

"It takes a lot of planning to do it right, and that is what I do."

She smiled down at him as he looked up at
her. Slowly, her smile began to fade as they
looked into each other's eyes. He reached out
and gently put his hands on her narrow waist.
Carefully, almost as if she would break if he
moved too quickly, he turned and guided her
around while lowering her down onto his lap.
She wrapped her arms around his neck as she
sat down. As he put his arms around her
narrow waist, she looked down at his face.
She lowered her face to meet his and their lips
met in a soft and loving kiss.

Their kiss lasted for almost a full minute.
It was not a heavy passionate kiss, but rather a
loving and gentle kiss. A warm kiss that came
from deep down in the heart, a kiss that was
meant to tell them of their love for each other.

As the kiss ended, she leaned back away
from him a little and looked into his eyes. She
felt his love for her in that warm, gentle kiss,
in his deep dark brown eyes and in his caring
smile. It left no doubt in her mind that he
loved her. She leaned down and rested her
head on his shoulder. She was more than

satisfied to just be sitting on his lap and wrapped in his arms.

Tony held her close to him, simply enjoying the closeness of her. He could smell the scent of her hair as it mixed with the soft, light fragrance of the soap she had bathed with. He could not help but think how nice she smelled and how warm she felt.

After several minutes, she sat up straight and looked down at him. There was a soft smile of contentment on her lips, those same lips that had warmed his heart just a few minutes earlier. It quickly changed to a devilish grin.

"Did you know it is snowing again?" she asked.

There was a hint of excitement in her voice. It was as if she had become an excited teenager again.

"No. Very hard?"

"No, not really. Would you like to go for a walk in the snow before we have dinner?"

"Sure. Why not."

Tony could not resist spending time with her. It was the first time that he had seen her so bubbly and excited about life.

"Good. Then put this stuff away and let's get ready."

Marcie gave him a quick kiss and got up off his lap. She turned toward him and held out her hands. He took her hands, stood up in front of her, leaned down and kissed her lightly on the forehead.

Tony put his arm around behind her as they walked out of the study and up the stairs. At the top of the stairs, he turned her in front of him and put his arms around her waist.

"Dress warm," he said as he looked into her beautiful blue eyes.

"I will."

He took his arms from around her and watched her as she disappeared into her room. The door slowly closed in front of him, then he turned and went into his room.

"Some day she will come to me in my room," he said to himself as he closed the door.

Marcie changed into a pair of jeans and one of the sweatshirts. As she sat on the edge of the bed and slipped on her snow boots, she glanced out the window. The snow was still falling. She smiled to herself as she remembered falling in the snow on her back and making snow angels on the front yard of the big white house where she lived when she was a small girl.

She felt a sudden pang of guilt. The news media had reported her as missing, and it was more then likely that the national news had picked up the story and broadcasted it across the country. She needed to call home and let her folks know that she was safe.

Marcie quickly stood up and ran for the door. The door flew open as she pulled at it. Seeing Tony standing in front of her caused her to stop suddenly and look at him.

"I have to call my mother."

The urgency in her voice startled Tony. He did not know what to say so he simply motioned toward the stairs and let her go ahead of him. By the time he reached the bottom of the stairs, she was already dialing the phone. He watched her as she listened for an answer. The look on her face showed the pain in her heart. It took him a minute to realize just what had caused this sudden change in her. As soon as she began to talk to her mother and her face showed the relief she was feeling, he closed the door to the dining room to give her some privacy.

Tony sat down in the living room and waited for her to finish talking with her mother. As soon as she finished, she came into the living room and sat down beside him. The look on her face showed the relief that she was feeling.

"Everything okay?"

"Everything's just fine. I told her that I would have to stay here for awhile, but I would come home as soon as possible."

"I'm glad. Do you still want to go for that walk?"

"Yes," she replied with a grin.

"There is a little restaurant just a few blocks from here. It's not very fancy, but the food is good and there's lots of it. What do you say we go there for dinner?"

"I don't get very many chances to eat in little out of the way restaurants. It sounds kind of cozy. Let's go."

Tony found it a pleasant relief to find someone who liked the simple things and did not have to be taken to the finest eating places in town to have a good time. He stood up and reached out to her. She took his hand and stood up in front of him. He took her in his arms, leaned down and kissed her lightly.

Marcie liked the way he made her feel special. The tenderness of his kiss made her love him even more. She liked to be in his strong arms and held close to him.

Tony pulled back a little and looked down at her. He did not want to let go of her, but his head was telling him to slow down. He had already had two relationships that were less than perfect. He really needed to know this woman a lot better. It was one thing to help her, but quite another to become deeply involved with her.

Tony let go of her and turned toward the closet. As he was getting their coats, Marcie wondered why he had pulled away from her so quickly. She could not think of anything she had done. Was he having second thoughts about her? Was he not really sure how he felt about her? Was he suddenly afraid to get involved with her and her problems?

Marcie was sure that he was not afraid to get involved with her problems because he had already proved that he wanted to help her with them. The only thing left was that he was afraid to get involved with her, but why?

Tony held out her coat for her. She turned around as she slid her arms into the selves. She did not turn back around to look at him while she zipped up her coat and wrapped her scarf around her neck. Her insecurities were coming back. She wondered if he really liked her or if he was just being kind to her.

Marcie was no longer sure that she wanted to go for this walk with him. She felt a sudden urge to return to her room and just stay there.

"Are you ready?" Tony asked.

She turned around to face him. She wanted to ask him what was wrong with her that he did not want her, but decided that might be a big mistake.

"Yes," she replied softly.

Tony reached over and opened the door. He watched Marcie as she stepped out onto the porch. He was sure that he had caused her to wonder about him with his sudden release of her.

Marcie looked out toward the park as she waited for him to lock the door. She glanced up at him as he reached out and took her hand in his. She did not know what to think now, but she was glad that he took hold of her hand. It gave her some encouragement that he was not rejecting her completely. It was clear to her that he was thinking about something and she needed to give him time to decide what it was he wanted, too.

Silently, they walked along the sidewalk in the fresh snow. It was cold, but Marcie was not feeling the cold from the weather. She wanted to talk to Tony, but did not know just what to say.

Tony was deep in his own thoughts. Why had he suddenly backed away from her? She had been warm and caring toward him. She had given him no reason to think that she was anything like his ex-wife, or his ex-girlfriend.

As they turned the corner toward the restaurant, Tony had convinced himself that she was not like the others. She was not only different, but she was very special. Maybe he should be a little careful and give their relationship a chance. After all, they had not known each other but a couple of days. With that decision made in his mind, he squeezed her hand gently.

Marcie felt his gentle squeeze of her hand. That simple touch reassured her that he was with her again. He had come back to her from wherever his mind had taken him and he was thinking about her again.

CHAPTER ELEVEN

It wasn't very long before they arrived at the corner restaurant. Tony opened the door for Marcie. She walked in and looked around. It was a small restaurant with a long counter on one side of the room and several booths on the other. It had a cozy atmosphere. Although the place was quite old, it was clean and well maintained. Some of the pictures on the walls dated back to before Marcie was even born.

Tony followed Marcie through the door. As he moved up behind her, he placed his hand on the small of her back and gently guided her to an empty booth in the back. There were several people at the counter, and a couple of the booths were occupied. When they reached an empty booth, Tony helped Marcie remove her coat and hung it on the coat hook next to the booth.

"Hey, Tony. How yah been?"

Tony turned around and looked toward the kitchen. Leaning against the chrome shelve was an older man with gray hair and a white chef's hat.

"Pretty good, Sam. How about yourself?"

"Ah, you know me. Can't complain."

Tony turned back around and noticed that Marcie was smiling up at him. Tony slid into the booth across from her.

"You come here a lot?" Marcie asked.

"I used to come here a couple of times a month, but it's been awhile."

"It's been a long time, Tony."

Marcie and Tony looked up at the rather large woman standing next to the table holding two menus in her hand. The woman was wearing a red apron over a white waitress uniform. Her hair was gray and the lines in her face showed she had not had an easy life, but the sparkle in her eyes said that she was happy.

"Nellie, you look as beautiful as ever. It really is good to see you again," Tony said with a smile.

"You always could spread it on thick," she replied with a deep laugh. "Are you hungry?"

Tony looked over at Marcie while Nellie set the menus down in front of them. He was feeling hungry, but was not sure about Marcie.

"How about some coffee while you make up your minds?"

"That would be great, Nellie."

"I know you like yours black. How do you like your coffee, Miss?"

"Black would be fine, thank you," Marcie replied.

"Two coffees, black," Nellie said as she turned and walked toward the counter.

Marcie picked up the menu in front of her and began looking through it. Although Tony seemed to be looking at his menu, she sensed that he was watching her. She looked over the top of the menu.

"What would you recommend?" Marcie asked.

"Sam makes a great Swiss Steak. The sauce he uses is his own creation, but you better be hungry if you order it."

Marcie smiled as she looked at Tony. When she had first come in with him, she felt that he had distanced himself from her, but now he seemed to have come back to her again.

"I'll have the Swiss Steak," she said bravely.

Tony smiled back at her. "Me, too."

Just as they were putting the menus on the edge of the table, Nellie returned with their coffee.

"Have you decided?"

"Yes. We'll have the Swiss Steak."

"Good. Two Swiss Steak platters."

Tony watched Nellie as she walked away, then turned his attention to Marcie. He glanced down at her hand on the table. He reached across the table and put his hand over hers.

Marcie looked across the table at a man she hardly knew. Yet, she knew that she loved him. The warmth of his hand over hers and the warmth of his smile touched her heart. It just seemed right to be here with him.

Tony was looking into her blue eyes. She was so pretty and he desired her so much that it made him a little leery. He was going to have to come to terms with his own feelings.

He could not understand why he was so hesitant about letting her know how he felt about her. She had never asked anything of him, had made no effort to change him, and seemed to accept him just the way he was.

Tony's fingers gently slid over the soft skin on the back of Marcie's hand as he thought about her. It was time to tell her how he felt. He did not want her to return to Ohio or Nashville, but wanted her to stay here in Denver with him. They could deal with whatever kind of lawsuit her promoter threw at them.

"Marcie, I - -."

"Two Swiss Steak Platters," Nellie interrupted. "Enjoy."

Tony looked up at Nellie's smiling face and sat back to give her room to set the plates on the table. He could not be angry with her. After all, she did not know he was about to tell the woman across the table from him that he loved her.

Marcie watched Tony as he thanked Nellie for the dinners. She wondered what it was he wanted to say before he was interrupted. She glanced across the table at Tony as she placed her napkin in her lap and picked up her dinnerware.

Marcie had gotten the feeling that Tony had wanted to talk to her earlier, but was not sure. He had been very quiet most of the way to the restaurant.

Tony unwrapped his dinnerware and placed his napkin in his lap. He looked across the table and smiled.

"Shall we eat?"

Marcie looked down at the plate. There was a lot of food on her plate, but it looked really good and she was hungry. She ate in silence hoping that Tony would tell her what was on his mind after dinner.

After they had eaten as much as they could, Tony sat back and sipped at his coffee. It had been a very good meal, but there was just too much to finish.

"I think the walk home will do us a lot of good tonight," Tony said with a sigh.

"I need to walk some of this dinner off, but I want to take my time at it."

"I think running is out of the question anyway," he said with a smile.

"Can I interest you is some desert?" Nellie asked.

Tony looked up at her and smiled. "Nellie, I'm sorry, but I don't have any room left for desert."

"I don't either," Marcie added.

"Can I get you some more coffee?"

"Yes, please," Tony replied.

Marcie watched as Nellie picked up the plates. As soon as Nellie left, Marcie put her hand out on the table. She hoped that Tony would hold her hand again and tell her what he was going to tell her before dinner.

Tony reached across the table and put his hand over hers again, but he did not say anything. He wanted to say something about how he felt about her and what he hoped she would do once everything with her contract was straightened out, but this was not the time or the place. Tony decided that he would wait until they were walking home.

"Thank you for coming, and it was good to see you again, Tony," Nellie said as she refilled their cups and gave Tony the check.

"Yeah, and don't be such a stranger," Sam called out from the kitchen.

"I won't," Tony promised.

"These people are almost like family to you, aren't they?" Marcie said.

"Yes, I guess they are. I used to eat here a lot after my divorce. I got to know them, and I guess they got to know me a little."

"They seem like really nice folks."

"They are. They gave me a lot of comfort during a difficult time."

Marcie sipped at her coffee. This little restaurant reminded her of a little cafe in her hometown. The people were friendly and everyone seemed to know everyone else. She realized that she had missed that in her life.

Tony finished his coffee and waited for Marcie. When she had finished, he gently squeezed her hand.

"Are you ready to go?"

"Yes."

Tony stood up and took Marcie's coat off the rack while Marcie slid out of the booth. He held her coat for her while she slipped her arms into the sleeves. She walked over toward the door and waited for Tony while he left a tip on the table and paid the check. He held the door for her and they left the restaurant.

Once outside, Tony slipped his arm around behind Marcie. They turned down the sidewalk and walked back toward Washington Park. It had stopped snowing and the ground was covered with a coating of fresh snow. They were the first to make tracks in the new snow.

The air was crisp and clear, and it was much colder than it had been before dinner. Tony looked up at the sky. While they had been in the restaurant, the sky had cleared and he could see the stars through the bare tree branches.

"I think it will be a nice day tomorrow. Maybe, I can show you around Denver. It really is nice when it's sunny," he said.

Marcie looked up at him and wondered if he was just being nice to her or if he had some hidden meaning behind what he had said. She turned away and looked straight ahead. She needed to hear him say that he wanted her to stay. She needed to hear that more than anything.

Tony squeezed her hand lightly and looked at her. His thoughts were turning over and over in his head. He wanted to take her in his arms and tell her not to go away. He needed to tell her that he cared about her very much. He knew he was going to tell her, but he was having difficulty getting the words out.

They walked silently along the sidewalk. Each wishing that the other would say something, anything to break the silence. The only sound was the muffled sounds of their boots as they shuffled through the snow.

Suddenly, Tony stopped and jerked Marcie around so she was standing directly in front of him. He grabbed her by the shoulders and looked into her eyes.

"Damn it, I don't want you to go," he blurted out at her.

For several seconds Marcie just looked at him. The suddenness of his action and the sharp tone of his voice had frightened her. But as his words began to soak in, she realized that he had said what she needed to hear.

Marcie threw her arms around him and held him tightly. Tony wrapped her is his arms. It was several minutes before they let loose of each other enough to be able to look at each other.

"What took you so long," she said smiling up at him.

"Kiss me," Tony said with a sigh of relief.

Marcie tipped her head to one side as Tony lowered his face to meet her. Their lips met in a loving kiss that warmed their hearts. Tony held her against him and savored this moment with her.

Reluctantly, Tony let go of her. He gently turned her around and tucked her under his arm as they once again walked down the sidewalk. They turned, crossed the street and entered the park. Leaning against each other, they slowly walked through the park leaving a trail in the snow where they had been.

As they walked around the pond, Marcie laid her head on Tony's shoulder. A feeling of contentment had come over her. At least for now, she could relax and enjoy this time with him. She did not have to think about what might happen tomorrow. Tomorrow was a long way away.

Tony stopped and looked up at the sky. The stars were still shining brightly and there was a ghostly ring around the moon. It was not the moon that he was thinking about, but rather the woman he had securely held at his side. Would it be possible for them to have a normal relationship? After all, she was a famous country singer and he was just a working stiff. Would she be happy spending the rest of her life here with him or would she miss the bright lights and the big crowds?

Marcie looked up at him. It was clear that he had something on his mind, but had chosen not to share it with her. The fact that he had decided not to share his thoughts with her made her wonder if he cared as much for her as she cared for him.

Slowly, Tony turned his head and looked down at her. She seemed concerned about something and he was sure he knew what she was worried about. He smiled as he reached out and put his hand on her cheek. He felt a slight shiver come from her as he touched her and his first thought was that she was getting cold.

"Are you cold?"

"A little."

"Maybe, we should go home," he suggested.

Marcie was a little puzzled as she looked at him. Was his reference to "home" just because it was his home or was there some other meaning? Perhaps he was indicating that it was their home? It suddenly occurred to her that she hoped he was referring to "their home", as she would like to make his home, "their home".

Tony removed his hand from her cheek, reached down and took her hand in his. They started to walk toward Tony's house, moving along a little faster then they had before.

Marcie was sure they were going faster because she had said she was getting cold.

As she walked at his side, her mind filled with questions that were hard for her to answer. She was in love with this man, but was he in love with her? She wanted to stay with him, but did he want to stay with her? He said he didn't want her to go, but did he really mean it?

Her thoughts were interrupted when Tony suddenly stopped her. She looked around and realized that he had just stopped her from stepping out into the street right into the path of an oncoming car. She looked up at him.

"Are you all right?"

Tony's voice showed his deep concern for her, and the look in his eyes showed how worried he was about her.

"Yes, ah - - I'm fine. I'm sorry. I wasn't paying attention, I guess."

Tony took her in his arms and held her close. He looked up as if to thank God that she was safe. As his gaze drifted down, he glanced across the street toward his house.

His gaze became fixed on a car parked in front of the house next door to his.

"Damn!" he said in frustration.

"What is it?" Marcie asked as she looked up at him.

"You see that red sports sedan parked over there?"

Marcie turned to look.

"Yes.   What about it?" she asked, not knowing why he was interested in the sports sedan.

"That's Linda's car."

"Are you sure?"

"Yes, I'm sure."

"What would her car be doing here?"

"I don't know."

Tony took Marcie's hand and they started across the street. He did not see anyone in the car. It made Tony wonder where Linda was and what she was doing in this neighborhood.

They walked up the sidewalk to the house. Just as they approached the porch, Linda stepped out from behind one of the large brick pillars on the porch.

"Well, I see you still have little Miss Hillbilly hanging on you," Linda said with a nasty sneer on her face.

"That will be enough out of you. What do you want?"

"Still protecting her, I see."

"Unless you have some papers to serve, I suggest that you get off my property."

Marcie stood by his side and looked at Linda. She had run into people like Linda before, all puffed up with their own importance, only this time she had had about enough.

"Miss Forrest, I don't know what your problem is, but if you continue to harass Mr. Beckman and myself at all hours of the day and night, I will file a complaint with the police. In my business, people sometimes become a real nuisance. I have learned how to deal with them. I don't see that you are any different. I seriously doubt that your law firm would like it very much if you were on the front page of the local paper for being arrested for harassment. Do you?" she asked as she waited for Linda to reply.

Linda just looked at Marcie. Up until now, Marcie had been the quiet and submissive type, but suddenly she was willing to fight back. Linda was not sure what to do now. It was clear that her law firm would not stand for her being on the front page of the paper, at least not for being arrested.

"I think that you better go before she gets really mad," Tony said trying not to let his pride in Marcie show too much.

Linda looked from Tony to Marcie, then back to Tony. The look on Marcie's face convinced her that Marcie meant what she said. Linda looked once again at Marcie, then turned and walked down the sidewalk to her car.

Tony and Marcie watched her as she walked away. Tony put his arm around Marcie's shoulder. She had stood her ground against Linda. He had always been sure that she had a certain spirit about her but that it had been buried under the slow build up of her problems with her attorney and promoter.

Marcie turned and looked up at Tony. Slowly, a smile came over her face. Her old confidence had returned. She once again felt alive and that there was really hope for the future.

"Shall we go in?" Tony asked with a grin.

"Yes," Marcie replied with a renewed confidence.

Tony reached in his pocket for his key. Marcie stood beside him as he unlocked the door and opened it for her, then Tony followed her into the house.

CHAPTER TWELVE

Tony was proud of Marcie for the way she stood up to Linda. She had a strong spirit that he admired. Yet, even with this feeling of pride in her, he couldn't keep from wondering why Linda had come to his house in the first place. His mind played with that thought as he took Marcie's coat and hung it up in the closet. He took off his coat and hung it beside her coat, but he was so deep in thought that he did not notice Marcie was watching him.

"What's the matter?" Marcie asked as she looked at him.

Tony could see the worry in her eyes as he reached out and took her hand. He wanted to ease her worry, but it was not going to be easy since he was a little worried, too.

"Sit down. I'll help you with your boots."

Marcie sat down on the chair while Tony knelt down in front of her. She waited for him to say something, anything. Instead he pulled off one boot and then the other. As he set her boots aside, Marcie reached down and touched him on the shoulder. He looked up at her.

"She wants you back, doesn't she?" Marcie asked. Her voice was so quiet that it would have been hard for anyone just a few feet away to hear her.

Tony looked into her eyes. He did not care what Linda wanted, but he could see it mattered very much to Marcie. He felt the need to reassure Marcie that he was no longer interested in Linda.

"I don't know what she wants, and I don't care what she wants. What I want is to be with you and have you stay here with me. I want you to be happy," he said softly as he looked at her face.

Marcie looked deep into his eyes. She was sure he meant what he said. It lifted her spirits and restored her confidence in herself, and she needed that right now.

Marcie leaned down toward Tony. When their lips met, they shared a warm, loving kiss that sent a peaceful sensation through her.

After their kiss, Tony leaned back and looked up at her. This was a very special woman, he thought. She was the kind of woman he needed in his life, but had not been able to find in the past.

Tony was about to tell Marcie that he cared very much about her and that he loved her, but the harsh ringing of the phone interrupted him. Marcie grinned at the disgusted look on Tony's face. It was the third time they had been interrupted at a romantic moment by that very phone.

"I think I'm going to have that phone ripped out," he said as he stood up and walked over to the phone.

"Hello."

"Hi. This is Jeff."

"Hi, Jeff. What's up?"

"What did you do, or say, to Linda?"

"What are you talking about?"

"She just called me on her cell phone. She said that Marcie threatened her and she's mad as hell."

"She sure got hold of you in a hurry."

"She called me from her car. What happened?"

"Listen Jeff, Marcie didn't threaten her. Well, she did in a way, but it wouldn't have happened if Linda hadn't been waiting for us on my front porch."

"What was Linda doing on your front porch?" Jeff asked.

"How should I know, she didn't bother to tell us why she was here."

Marcie stood up and walked over to Tony's side. She put her arm around him and watched him. Tony smiled down at her as he listened to Jeff. It was hard for him not to think that Linda had gone over the edge and was out of control.

"After Linda told me that Marcie had threatened her, she said that she would be serving you with papers for a lawsuit to the tune of five million dollars in the morning," Jeff said.

"She said that she was serving me?"

"Yes, that's what she said."

"Did she say I was the one being sued, or Marcie?"

"She said you, Tony."

"What the hell can she sue me for?" Tony asked, puzzled by what Jeff had told him.

"Nothing I know of. I think she's lost it. She must have meant Marcie. It was my understanding that Marcie's promoter was the one filing the lawsuit and that Linda would simply be serving it."

"Mine, too," Tony replied.

"She can't seem to keep it straight as to who is suing who. I wouldn't worry about it. I'll call her law firm. I'm going to have a talk with her boss about her conduct. If he doesn't pull her off this case, I'm going to suggest that a little conflict of interest charge might just be leveled against her and his firm with the Bar Association. I don't think it will come to that, but a little arm twisting won't hurt."

"I hope you don't have to go that far."

"Yeah, me, too. By the way, I have a call into Marcie's lawyer's office in Nashville. It seems that her attorney is looking forward to talking to me after all. He wasn't at first, but when I suggested that there was a very strong possibility of a counter suit for malpractice coming his way, he decided that he might want to talk to me tomorrow morning. I get the impression that he would like to avoid a malpractice suit."

"Great."

"Don't celebrate yet. We are not out of the woods, but it looks like we might be getting out onto the playing field. Tell Marcie that I'll call her after I talk to him."

"I will. Talk to you later," Tony said, then hung up the phone.

"I take it that was Jeff?" Marcie asked.

"It was, and things are looking up. Your attorney has agreed to talk, thanks to a little persuasion from Jeff."

"That's great."

"Jeff will be calling after he talks to your attorney in Nashville, or should I say your ex-attorney."

Marcie smiled up at Tony. She had been hopeful that Jeff would be able to help her get out of her contract. Now there was a light at the end of what had seemed like a very long and very dark tunnel.

Tony leaned over and kissed her on the forehead as he gave her a big hug. Things were beginning to fall into place. Marcie was going to be able to decide just what it was she really wanted. She was going to have to start making some decisions for herself.

Tony was happy that Marcie was going to be able to take charge of her life again, but at the same time he had some reservations. What if she decided to go back to Nashville and resume her singing career? What if she decided to go back to Ohio and just start all over again? Could she be happy staying here with him? Maybe, it was a little early to be worrying about what she might do since there was still the possibility of a very large lawsuit still looming on the horizon.

Marcie could see that Tony was thinking very hard about something. She could understand, after all, she had a lot of things running through her mind as well. She had a very good career in the music business, but was she really ready to give it up for this man? It was going to take her some time to figure out just what she wanted out of her life. It struck her as just a little funny, but she had run away in the first place to make that very decision and she still was trying to make it.

"How about a cup of coffee?" Tony asked.

"Sure," she replied as she looked up and smiled at him.

Tony gave her a squeeze and together they went into the kitchen. Marcie got a couple of coffee mugs while Tony made a small pot of coffee.

Marcie sat down at the table and watched Tony. She was noticing that he was a handsome man who seemed to be very confident in himself. He seemed to know what he wanted and could find a way to get it. If he was so confident in himself, why was he having such a hard time letting her know that he loved her? She was sure that he loved her, but why wouldn't he tell her so?

"Tony?"

"Yes?" he replied as he turned in response to the urgency that was in the sound of her voice.

"What do you think I should do?" she asked as she looked at him.

She knew her question was one that only she could answer, but she was hoping that Tony would tell her to stay with him again, not to return to Nashville. More importantly, she needed to hear him say that he loved her.

"About what?"

Marcie just looked at him. She could not believe that he was so dense. She was trying to make the most important decision of her life and he was not helping her.

"About my life," she blurted out at him.

"I can't tell you what to do."

Tony's response simply increased her frustration. It was clear that he was not going to try to influence her in any way. He had told her once that he wanted her to stay, but in the end it was going to have to be her decision.

Marcie wanted to share her life with this man, yet he was not going to make it easy for her. His apparent lack of interest in helping her infuriated her. She slowly stood up while she stared at him.

"Damn you," she said then quickly turned and ran out of the room.

"Marcie!" Tony called out after her.

Tony couldn't figure out what had set her off. He was just doing what she wanted, leaving her to make up her own mind, to make her own decisions. He had seen a spirit in her earlier this evening, but now she wanted him to tell her what to do. Tony was confused. He couldn't understand what made her so upset. This whole thing had been about her not having control of her own life.

He wanted to help her make up her mind. He wanted to tell her to stay with him. But it had to be her decision or nothing would have changed. After all, he had already told her that he didn't want her to leave, what more could he say?

He heard Marcie slam the door to her room. Tony thought about going after her, but decided that he would give her some time to herself, some time to think. Maybe, she would come around.

Tony went into the living room and sat down. He thought about turning on the television to watch the news, but he didn't really care what was going on in the rest of the world. He had enough going on right here in his little piece of it to keep him busy.

Tony leaned back in his chair and closed his eyes. He had never met a woman quite like Marcie. She was beautiful, anyone could see that, but she was something else. Under all that confusion and lost trust, there was a woman that could excite him like no other woman he had ever met. She was a woman who could make him happy by just being near him. There was something very much alive about her. He had seen it a few brief times while he was with her.

It was close to midnight when Tony realized that it had been at least three hours since Marcie had gone to her room. He was sure that if she had not come downstairs by now, she was not going to come down at all tonight.

He got up and locked up the house. After shutting off the lights, he went upstairs to his bedroom. He got ready for bed, then climbed into the big feather bed. He lay looking up at the ceiling, wondering what was going on in the room across the hall.

* * * *

Marcie ran into her room and shut the door. She threw herself onto the bed and buried her face in the pillow and cried. Gradually, she began to regain her composure and rolled over on her back. She hugged the pillow to her breasts as she looked up at the ceiling. Her thoughts began to come more clearly.

She began to realize that Tony had been doing just what she had asked him to do. He had given her the time and space to decide for herself just what it was that she wanted. Tony had been very careful not to interfere. In fact, he had been a little too careful as far as she was concerned. He had not tried to tell her what to do, or even hinted at what she should do. He had made every effort to give her the opportunity to choose her own course.

Now it was time for her to make her own choices. She was going to have to decide what she wanted, what her options were, and how she was going to get what she wanted.

It was time to start answering those questions that only she could answer. The first question that she had to answer was did she want to go back to Nashville and get her music career started up again? No, she didn't want to do that. She didn't want to have to deal with the promoters, lawyers, and especially the one-night stands all over the country. She had had enough of that kind of a life style.

"What kind of a life do you want?" she asked herself out loud.

It was not all that easy a question for her to answer. The only life styles she had known were that of a kid in a sort of mid-class family, and that of a country western singer on the road most of the time. She knew that there had to be something better than the latter.

Marcie wiped the tears from her face with the corner of the pillowcase and sat up. She looked over toward the dresser mirror. Her hair was a mess, and she didn't think that she looked very appealing to a man.

"Do you think you would be happy taking care of a man, a man like Tony?" she asked her reflection.

As she ran her hand through her hair, she thought about her question. Would she really be taking care of him or would he be taking care of her? Maybe, it would be a lot of both of them taking care of each other. Now that idea appealed to her.

She sat back down on the bed and tried to picture Tony with her and a child. Somehow, she was sure that Tony would like kids. She had often thought about having a family and wondered if Tony would want a family.

She let herself flop backwards on the bed. The idea of being a wife and mother was one of those things she had kept locked up in the back of her mind. It had always been there, but now seemed like the perfect time to bring it out in the open and really think about it. She closed her eyes and let her mind wonder for a few minutes.

Suddenly, she remembered what Tony had said earlier. He had told her that he wanted her to stay. It had not been stated very eloquently, or even very romantically. He had simply blurted it out. Never the less, in his own way he had told her that he wanted her here with him. It may not have been a proposal of marriage, but it was certainly a start.

In the next instant, Marcie decided what she wanted. She wanted to settle down and raise a family. She wanted to raise that family with Tony, Tony Beckman.

Marcie no longer would ride a bus from one town to the next doing one night concerts. She would no longer answer to some promoter or lawyer she didn't trust, and didn't even like. Instead, she would go places with Tony. She would help him with his business when she could, and maybe someday go to PTA meetings.

She was sure that she was in love with Tony and equally sure that he loved her. The big question now was how was she going to get him to ask her to marry him?

Since he was not going to help her make decisions, she was going to have to make them herself. After all, she was a woman, and women were supposed to be able to get men to do anything. At least that's what she had heard.

Marcie sat up on the edge of the bed and looked in the mirror. If she was going to get her man, then it was time for her to begin looking like the woman that Tony would like to have at his side, a woman with confidence and spirit.

With her new resolve, she stood up and began undressing. She went into the bathroom and took a warm soothing shower and washed her hair. After drying off, she wrapped herself in a large bath towel and dried her hair with the hair dryer that Tony had left in the bathroom for her.

As she combed out her hair, she noticed that a certain glow had returned to her face. She was feeling much more confident. It was almost as if the weight of the world had been lifted from her shoulders. She smiled at the reflection of herself. She had decided what she wanted and she was getting ready to go after it.

Marcie picked up her lipstick and looked into the mirror. She wished she had picked up some other makeup, but why? Tony had fallen in love with her without all her stage makeup, what was the need for it now. She was no longer going to be on stage for anyone. Tony liked her the way she looked now. She smiled at her reflection as she put on just a little lipstick.

Marcie stepped back away from the mirror and removed the towel from around her body, letting it drop to the floor. She picked up the light blue nightgown that Tony had insisted she buy. She held it up in front of herself and looked at the mirror. It was a pretty nightgown and she was sure that Tony would like to see her wearing it.

She put her arms inside the nightgown and raised it up over her head. She let it fall down over her head and cascade on down over her slender body. The soft material felt cool against her bare skin.

Looking into the mirror, she straightened out the nightgown and was pleased with the way it clung to her body. The lacy bodice with the deep cut V neckline showed off her round firm breasts while the narrow waist helped to accent the smooth flowing lines of her hips. Marcie could not keep herself from staring at the woman in the mirror. She had never thought of herself as being attractive and certainly not sexy, but here she was looking at a very attractive and even sexy woman.

Her thoughts were disturbed by the sound of the door across the hall closing. She realized that Tony must have decided not to wait for her to make a decision tonight, but decided to go to bed. It had not occurred to her that she might have to confront him with her decision in his bedroom.

She turned and looked at the door. Should she go ahead and go to him in his bedroom, or should she simply go to bed and talk to him in the morning? She let out a sigh of disappointment as she sat down on the edge of the bed. She had been ready to stand up in front of him and tell him that she loved him and that she wanted to stay here in Denver with him if he would have her. But now he was in his bedroom, one of the few places in the house that she felt was his and his alone.

Marcie sat with her head hung down and her shoulders slumped in disappointment looking down at the floor as she tried to think. Her mind helped her visualize his bedroom with its western art on the walls, the antique furniture, an old chest at the foot of the bed and that large four-poster feather bed.

It was the thought of the feather bed that caused her to sit up. She remembered how that room had made her feel, warm and comfortable. The more she thought about Tony's bedroom, the more she wanted it to be their bedroom. Why shouldn't she be in that room with him? The room was more a part of Tony than any other part of the house, except for maybe his study.

Marcie stood up and went to the door. She reached out and took hold of the doorknob and turned it. As she opened the door, she noticed that the hall was dark. Tony had closed up the house for the night. She shut off the light in her room and stepped across the hall to the door to Tony's bedroom. She reached out and took hold of the doorknob, but hesitated.

CHAPTER THIRTEEN

Tony heard Marcie just outside his door. He was not sure if he should get up and see what she wanted or just stay in bed. He hoped that she was going to come to him, but felt that was not likely. He decided she was probably feeling thirsty and was going downstairs to get something to drink. It crossed his mind that she might have decided to leave, although something in the recesses of his mind told him that she wouldn't sneak out in the middle of the night.

Tony listened very carefully. He heard the slight squeak of the doorknob being turned and looked over toward the door. Slowly, the door began to open. There was a little light coming in the window from a streetlight outside. He could barely see Marcie in the doorway. He could see that she was wearing the sheer nightgown.

"Are you awake?" Marcie asked softly.

She wanted him to hear her, but was almost wishing that he would not answer her. At least if he did not say anything, she would not have to deal with her fear of being rejected tonight. She would be able to return to her room and put off this encounter until morning. She even thought that it might be better if she waited until breakfast, anyway.

"Yes. Do you need something?"

"No. Well, yes."

"What is it?"

Marcie could hear the concern in Tony's voice. She immediately realized that she had caused him to worry. She had not wanted to do that to him.

"I'm sorry. It can wait until morning."

"Marcie, wait. Please talk to me."

Tony thought about turning on a light, but decided against it. If she did not think he could see her, she might be more open to him, more willing to say what is on her mind.

"I,.....I just wanted to tell you that I made up my mind on what I want."

Tony wanted to ask her what she had decided, but was not sure he was going to like the answer. There was a long silence before he said anything.

"What have you decided?"

"I've decided...that I want....to....to....to stay here with you, if you want me?"

Marcie sort of blurted out the end of her sentence. She was embarrassed more with the difficulty she had in saying it, than with what she had said. In an effort to avoid his rejection, she turned and started back toward her room.

"Wait!" Tony called out. "Please don't go."

Marcie stopped and slowly turned around. She could not see his face, but she could see him in the dimly lit room. He was sitting up in that large four-poster feather bed.

"Come over here, please," he said softly.

Marcie slowly walked toward the bed. As she stepped up next to the bed, she could see that he was sitting up with the covers up to his waist. In the slight glow of the streetlight through the window, she could see that he did not have anything on above his waist. Even in the dim light, she could see how very handsome a man he was.

As she stood next to the bed, Tony looked at her in the nightgown. She was the most desirable woman he had ever seen. He wanted her to climb into bed with him, but only if she wanted to spend not just the night, but forever with him.

"Marcie, I love you. I want you to stay with me, live here with me."

"I love you, too," Marcie replied with a sigh of relief. He had finally said what she needed to hear. He had told her before that he wanted her to stay, but he had not said that he loved her. Now that he had said he loved her, she realized that all her worries and fears had been for nothing. He wanted her as much as she wanted him.

"Stay here with me tonight."

Tony's words were not a question, but rather a loving request. It was clear to Marcie that he not only loved her, but that he desired her as well.

Marcie stepped up closer to the bed. As she looked at him, she reached up and slipped the nightgown off her shoulders. Slowly, she let the nightgown slide down over the smooth lines of her body until it fell into a pile at her feet. She stepped out of the nightgown as

Tony lifted the covers for her so that she could climb into the bed beside him. As she curled up alongside him, he pulled the covers up over her.

The warmth of Tony's body against her, and the soft comfort of the feather bed, made Marcie feel as if this was where she belonged. With her head resting on Tony's shoulder and her arm across his chest, she was feeling more loved than she had ever felt in her life.

Tony's hand slipped around behind her. She looked up at him as he gently pulled her up across his chest. He pulled her face down toward him until their lips met. They kissed, and their passion and desire for each other grew until they could no longer resist the need for more of each other.

* * * *

Marcie slowly opened her eyes. The morning sunlight was slipping into the room around the edges of the curtains, giving the room a soft glow. She smiled to herself as she thought of last night. She now knew what it was like to make love on a feather bed, and to sleep on one. It didn't matter to her if it was the bed or the loving last night that gave her this feeling. She was loved and that was what was important.

She could feel the warmth of Tony's body as he lay curled up against her back. He had one arm wrapped under her breasts and a hand gently cupping one of her breasts. She could feel his breath against her hair. She was sure that as long as she had his love, she would not have to worry about the Frank Alexanders of the world.

Marcie gently stroked Tony's arm. It was a strong arm and she felt so secure with it wrapped around her. She closed her eyes to help her savor this quiet, peaceful moment.

Tony felt her hand stroking his arm. He knew that she was awake, but he did not want to disturb her if she was deep in thought. He did not want to disturb the warm softness of her body against him, either. He was sure he could stand to wake up every morning for the rest of his life with this woman in his arms.

Marcie could sense that Tony was awake now. She slid her hand over his hand and pressed his hand firmly against her breast.

"I love you, Tony Beckman."

"I love you, Miss Marcie Roberts," he replied as he squeezed her tightly. "Are you ready to get up?"

"Mmmmmm, I don't think so," she murmured as she enjoyed his loving touch.

"Well, I have to get up."

Reluctantly, Marcie rolled away from him onto her stomach. Tony rolled out of bed on the other side and went into the bathroom. When he came back out, Marcie was still lying on her stomach almost completely uncovered. Tony sat down on the edge of the bed, reached out and gently touched her back.

"That feels good," she said in a soft quiet whisper.

Tony began rubbing her back. He slowly moved his hand from her shoulders, down her spine to the small of her back. It was impossible for him not to admire the smooth flowing lines of her naked body. He gently ran his hand over her butt and down onto her firm shapely legs.

"You are beautiful," he said as he looked at her.

Marcie rose up on her elbows and turned to look at him. "You are beautiful, too."

Tony rolled her over onto her back and laid down over her. She quickly wrapped her arms around him and held him tightly. Their lips met in a deep passionate kiss.

After several minutes, Tony rose up and looked down into her blue eyes. They were both breathing rather hard.

"I love you, and I want you to marry me."

Marcie looked up at him. She wanted to say "Yes" more than anything in the world, but was he ready to take on a five million dollar lawsuit?

Tony had a pretty good idea what was going on in Marcie's mind and why she was hesitant in answering him. If she would not come out and say what was making her hesitate, he would say it.

"Listen, I love you. No lawsuit, no fat cat lawyer or big shot promoter with his gorillas is going to stop me from marrying you. The only way you are going to get out of marrying me is for you, and only you, to say, "No"."

Slowly, a smile came over Marcie's lips.

"Since you put it that way, how can I refuse? Yes, I will marry you, but you have to promise to love me."

"Ah, finally, a promise I can really put my whole heart into."

Tony leaned down to kiss her again, but once again he was interrupted by the harsh sound of his telephone ringing.

"Damn it. This better be important," he said as he reached over to the nightstand for the phone. He hesitated for just a second before picking up the phone. He did not want to speak too harshly to someone on the other end, especially with the possibility that it might be one of his clients.

"Hello."

"Hi. I hope I didn't catch you at an inconvenient time?"

"Jeff? What the hell time is it? Isn't this just a little early for you?"

"Yes, it's a little early for me, but I have some news that I didn't think you'd want me to keep to myself any longer then necessary.

"It seems there's a big time difference between here and Nashville, well at least a big enough one that I got a call from there already this morning."

"Ah, Jeff. Would it be possible for you to get to the point?"

"Well, I would really like to drag this out as long as possible," Jeff replied with a hint of laughter in his voice.

"Jeff, get to the point," Tony demanded.

"Well, okay. It seems that Miss Roberts's lawyer has decided that it is in his best interest, and the interest of his firm, not to pursue any legal action against Miss Roberts. He has also convinced Mr. Alexander to drop any action that he might decide to take, or he might find himself a promoter without anyone to promote. How's that?"

"Jeff, you are terrific."

"I'm glad to see that you appreciate my talents. Would you be so kind as to inform Miss Roberts that she no longer has a contract, and that she is free to do as she pleases?"

Tony had been holding the phone so that Marcie could hear the conversation.

"I heard every beautiful word you said. And Jeff, thanks for everything."

"You are more than welcome, Miss Roberts."

"Please, call me Marcie. I think you will be seeing a lot of me around here."

"Are you staying here in Denver?" he asked with a hint of surprise in his voice.

"Yes, she is, Jeff," Tony said.

"I don't want to jump the gun, but might congratulations be in order?"

"They are," Marcie said hardly able to contain herself.

"Will you be singing around here?"

"No, Jeff. She will sing for me, only for me."

Tony set the phone in its cradle as he leaned down toward her.

"Kiss me," he said softly.

"With pleasure," she replied as she wrapped her arms around his neck and drew him down over her.

www.ingramcontent.com/pod-product-compliance
Lightning Source LLC
Chambersburg PA
CBHW071128170626
46809CB00002B/540